HIS ANGEL

"That is because you are gracious, generous, and kind, my dear. If you were to deck yourself out in the latest modes, you would leave the competition far behind."

Cordelia's blush rebloomed. "What silly flattery! I lack almost every quality expected in a reigning beauty."

"Why, Miss Bransford, I disagree." He continued. "If I might be so bold, you have superior attributes in all regards. Your hair is lovely, highlighted in gold. Your brow is wide and smooth, your eyes the color of a sunny sky—"

Her head snapped up. "Stop! I have never heard anything so preposterous."

"You have a saucy streak, which is charmingly contrary to your angelic countenance. Your figure is perfect—"

"Please, Lord Matthew, you have quite sufficiently proved your command of flummery and nonsense."

He had never seen her so lovely, eyes flashing, almost shaking with indignation. "I mean every word I spoke."

D1115239

Other Books by Victoria Hinshaw

THE FONTAINEBLEAU FAN

THE ELIGIBLE MISS ELLIOTT

MISS PARKER'S PONIES

MISS MILFORD'S MISTAKE

AN IDEAL MATCH
(Coming in November 2004)

Published by Zebra

CORDELIA'S CORINTHIAN

Victoria Hinshaw

ZEBRA BOOKS
KENSINGTON PUBLISHING CORP.
http://www.kensingtonbooks.com

One

If Miss Cordelia Bransford were to have the happiest summer of her life, she would have to prove herself smarter than a pheasant hen. She closed the copy of *Aesop's Fables* but kept her finger tucked in at "The Fox and the Pheasants." She leaned her head back against the soft squabs of the gently rocking coach and smiled to herself. How well the moral of the ancient tale applied to her situation. The poor pheasants worried so much about the danger from a fox lurking below their perch that they fell off, right into his jaws. Like those pheasants, if Corey let her fears about the future dominate her thinking, she was likely to fall prey to every form of misery her fertile imagination could concoct.

That she could not allow!

Corey intended to begin the most blissful time of her life when she arrived at her cousin Elaine's estate, perhaps her very last carefree summer. Her need to find a paid position next autumn, money to be able to send her parents to Bath, the fate of her feckless brother—all these things she pledged to leave behind her and simply luxuriate in the opulent comforts of Lodesham Hall. Time enough to fret later. For now, having a wonderful summer in Dorset must eclipse her concerns about the future. Her cousin's letters were filled with descriptions of the verdant park and its half-tame deer herd, the sparkling river and its feeder streams that flooded the water meadows in the spring, the bountiful orchards and fertile kitchen gardens, and best of all, the luxuriant flower gardens with more than forty varieties of roses—a paradise Corey longed to explore. On warm afternoons, she and Elaine would sit amongst the blossoms reading to each other or counting butterflies. What utter bliss.

Corey's pleasure should have begun with this journey, if she had been able to keep her mind off her problems. Three days ago, the Earl of Lodesham's grand traveling coach arrived at the vicarage in Mitton Moorby. The entire village was astonished by the fine team of four matched bays and postilions in striking livery adorned with gold braid and long, waving feathers. The earl even sent along Fanny, one of his wife's maids, to attend Corey at the coaching inns each evening along the journey from Yorkshire to Dorset. Fanny was an efficient woman who spoke only when spoken to; her silence had left many, many hours of quiet during which Corey could not stop her thoughts from rambling.

To prevent more unhappy contemplation of her future, Corey tried to read. At first, she had trouble in the rocking coach, but when the roads improved and she became more accustomed to the movement, she found she enjoyed perusing the little volume she purchased as a gift for Elaine's children. She imagined herself sitting in a sunny nursery, perhaps some afternoon next week, reading a story to the sweet little cherubs.

Now, on the final leg of her journey, Corey took Aesop's advice, stifling her worries and allowing her anticipation to build. She recalled Elaine's enthusiastic descriptions of the idyllic countryside and gazed out at the pale green leaves of early springtime arching over the quiet lanes that led from Dorchester to Lodesham Hall.

When they turned in between ornate iron gates next to a lodge house, Corey tried to catch a glimpse of the house, but there was nothing to be seen but sweeping green lawns and an orderly line of trees bordering the long, curving drive. She lowered the coach window, oblivious to the cool wind, eager for her first view of the grand Palladian mansion described in five years' worth of letters from her cousin. When the gray stone edifice came into view, Corey gave a little sigh of admiration. The tall-columned portico was every bit as imposing as the Prince Regent's Carlton House in London.

At the foot of the shallow stairs leading to the ornate iron door, Corey remembered to wait for the footman before she climbed down from the coach. Once on the ground, she gazed up at the coffered ceiling of the porch, so far above her that the gilding of the design was barely visible.

"Miss Bransford? I bid you welcome to Lodesham Hall." An austere butler in funereal black spoke from the top step, his enhanced height dwarfing her. He perfectly matched the solemn dignity of the imposing pillars.

She fingered the threadbare cuffs of her green pelisse and felt his eyes appraise her little rabbit fur muff. What must he think of her shabby appearance?

"Thank you." The words almost stuck in her throat.

Leaving the baggage to Fanny and the footmen, the butler indicated the door with a minimal bow. "Please come in. I am Oakley, the earl's butler."

"Thank you, Oakley." Why had her store of words dried up as unexpectedly as her mouth and lips?

He waved her into the foyer, closing the door behind them. "The countess is resting. I will have Mrs. Newsome take you to her." With that he disappeared behind the wide staircase leading to the first floor.

Corey stared about her at the immense hall, its cold magnificence making her shiver. She crossed the black-and-white marble squares of the floor to a tall pier glass. It stood above a pink marble slab supported on the backs of winged beasts of some exotic variety. She gazed into the mirror, perturbed at the image facing her. Wind-reddened cheeks and a tangle of brown hair sticking out of her bonnet gave her a thoroughly rumpled mien, worsened by her blush of humiliation at how little she conformed to the character of Elaine's distinguished residence. Nor would any of the gowns she brought improve the situation. Sad to say, the newest and best item in her wardrobe could not hold a candle to her surroundings. Any hope she had of disguising her status as Elaine's poorest relation was thoroughly dashed.

In a matter of moments, Mrs. Newsome bustled into the room. Her broad, cheerful face lifted Corey's spirits.

"This way, miss." Her black skirts swishing, the housekeeper started up the stairs. "My poor lamb is lying down."

Poor lamb? Whatever did the woman mean?

Corey followed the plump figure past the formal rooms of the first floor up another flight of stairs to the bedchambers. Mrs. Newsome opened the third door and nodded Corey into a dimly lit boudoir.

When her eyes grew accustomed to the faint light,

Corey hastened to a chair near the daybed where Elaine lay covered by a light rug, her eyes closed.

Corey sat a moment, unwilling to speak and risk waking Elaine.

But Elaine slowly opened her eyes. "Corey, dearest, how kind of you to come." To Corey's surprise, Elaine gave a series of little sobs.

"Why, Elaine, you are weeping." Corey knelt beside the bed and hugged Elaine to her. "Whatever is the matter?"

"Oh, I am sadly distraught. It is really nothing. Perry says I should be the happiest of women, but I do not agree. I can hardly bring myself to stand."

Corey released her and knelt beside the daybed. "But why? Are you ill?"

The tears trailed down Elaine's cheeks. "Quite the contrary. I am increasing again. Little Lawrence is still with the wet nurse, not nearly weaned."

"Your sensibilities are too refined, darling Elly. Perry is correct. You should be elated, not indulging in tears."

"But think of it. Four children in five years of marriage. I am tired."

"Of course you are, dearest. You are quite right in keeping to your bed." Corey glanced around the room. Even in the dimness, the elegance of the gold furniture, the supple softness of the thick carpet, the rose shade masking the lamp—all coalesced as a retreat of remarkable comfort.

But Elaine was anything but comfortable, grasping at Corey's hand. "I am especially glad you came, cousin dear. You see, our head nurse left last week, called away to her own mother's bedside. What could I say? Of course I had to let her go."

"Of course." Corey nodded in sympathy.

"Now there is no one to tend the children, except that imbecilic nursery maid who is barely able to keep the bedding clean. And I am not up to interviewing anyone for the post. I pray you will not mind checking on the children from time to time."

"I will be happy to see to them." Corey's quick response came without showing the hesitation she felt. "But I know very little of caring for children."

"I am sure you will be more than capable. Oh, my darling Corey, I shall make it up to you. When I feel better, I promise we will have a happy time together. Now, go get settled and come back to me later. I will have Bess bring the children to meet you then."

Corey hugged Elaine. "My dear, I only hope you soon improve, for your own sake. Do not worry about me."

Mrs. Newsome directed Corey to a large and airy room with walls covered in pale blue watered silk. A blue counterpane heavily embroidered with white roses and green leaves covered the wide bed beneath a canopy of white ruffles. Corey turned to exclaim to Mrs. Newsome of the beauty of the bedchamber, but swallowed her words when she saw the troubled expression on the housekeeper's face.

"Is there something wrong, Mrs. Newsome?"

"It's Lady Lodesham, miss. All of us 're troubled. We're hoping you'll do her good. She's sadly downcast, cries for hours. And little Henry and Gina, they see their mama crying and they don't understand. Sometimes they be downright naughty 'n' poor Bess, she don't do well with 'em. Maggie, the best maid in the house, is the only one who makes 'em mind. And I can hardly spare her, what with company here, and if her ladyship knew, she would not approve of Maggie tending the little ones. I hope you, being kin, can smooth things, miss."

Corey listened with growing chagrin. "I shall do my best, Mrs. Newsome. "But I . . ."

"Oh, Miss Bransford, it really wasn't my place to say all that. I 'pologize. It's just I feel so sorry for the countess and those little mites. And no one to go visit that poor little Lawrence in the village. It ain't right."

Corey forced a smile. "Now do not worry. We will sort out everything and even get Lady Lodesham back on her feet."

"Thank you, miss. I hoped you'd be a good influence. Her ladyship needs a friend."

As Mrs. Newsome left, Fanny came in and curtsied. "I will unpack your things now, miss."

Corey stopped herself from sending the maid away. In the last few nights, Fanny had seen enough of her linen to know its quality was not exactly up to the present setting. "Thank you, Fanny."

Corey walked to the window and pushed aside the sheer drapery. She would not mind tending Elaine's little son and daughter now and then, though she had no experience whatsoever beyond watching children in the care of other people. Besides reading to them, what did people do with children? She remembered playing with her dolls when she was little, but other than her own, childhood was a mystery.

In mere moments, Fanny finished placing Corey's things in the clothes press, then gathered several gowns over her arm. "I'll press these and hang them back here in an hour, miss."

"I appreciate that, Fanny."

The maid curtsied again and left the room, closing the door behind her.

Corey gazed outside at the smooth green expanse of grass in the park. Elaine's melancholy seemed a knotty obstacle to Corey's idyllic summer. The long, invigorating walks Corey envisioned with Elaine now seemed more likely to be taken at the pace of a two-year-old.

The blows had Matt reeling.

"Enough?" His opponent's voice was raspy and deep.

"No. Keep on." Captain Lord Matthew Allerton's breath came in short spurts. His balance was entirely off, his leg nearly buckling. He threw a punch but felt only the wind whistle past his arm.

Instantly he felt a jab to his jaw, a fist in his stomach. He tried to swing again and succeeded only in losing the last of his equilibrium. His leg collapsed beneath him and he thrust out an arm to break his fall.

But strong arms grabbed at him and kept him upright.

"How long?" he gasped.

"Seven minutes, milord."

"Confound it, Joseph. Not nearly enough."

Joe helped him to a bench outside the sparring ring. "Naw. But better."

Matt drew a deep, shuddering breath. None of Joe's taps had been hard enough to bruise, but his leg was simply too weak to keep him on his feet.

"Sadly, time has expired. I no longer can put them off. We meet today to set our departure date."

"Yer best bet is to throw a quick series—left, right down low, left agin. Finish 'em in three, four minutes flat."

Matt wished he were capable of taking care of his

old friends so neatly. "It is not as though they are weaklings or missing techniques. But your help has been invaluable, Joseph."

"Any time, milord." He saluted and joined another group of men across the room.

Matt listened to his breaths grow calmer. He was entirely disappointed in himself. *By God, I have to win. And I cannot sit out any phase of the competition, not without an explanation.*

He wiped the sweat from his face. His leg throbbed from his toes to his hip as if his wound stretched the distance instead of being centered in the muscle of his thigh just above his knee. Why did the pain and weakness continue a year after the battle? At this rate, he would be a grizzled old man before he conquered his limp. He could never tolerate being an invalid. He must regain every degree of his strength. Otherwise, who was he?

Matt gritted his teeth and massaged his thigh, willing the soreness away. His confounded infirmity did not bode well for success at Perry's gathering, the reunion of the Quorn Quartet's Corinthian competitions. Matt hoped the four old friends, comrades since their childhood, would enjoy each other's company as much as they had before Perry's marriage. They had met informally, but this would be a full-fledged resumption of what had been annual contests, the first since they had abducted Perry from his honeymoon and held him for almost an entire day and night before returning him to his bride.

The memory brought on a grin. What a devil of a fuss there had been! The new Countess of Lodesham had indulged in impressive hysterics.

He stood and the sharpness of the pain jerked him

back to his dilemma. How could he compete with the others when his leg hardly held him up after a few rounds? But he would not give in, not to the pain, not to the other men. He would compete, and he would win! Whether the competition was with rod and reel, with fists, on horseback, at bow and arrow or billiards, Matt would not allow himself to drop out for any reason whatsoever. That was final!

Constant exercise to strengthen his leg, that was what he needed to continue. Daily walks, just as Gentleman Jackson himself had suggested last week. Given the Quartet's penchant for late-night cards and wine, he should be able to rise early and slip away alone, never allowing them to find out the extent of his weakness. His pride had suffered quite enough in the past year. He would endure no more.

Forcing himself to walk without favoring his shaky leg, he found his valet and donned his street clothes.

In less than an hour, he joined Cedric and Alfred at the club for luncheon.

Cedric was adamant. "I say we leave tomorrow while the weather is fine. This time of year, the rain can last for days at a time."

Matt grinned to himself. Cedric, the Honorable Mr. Cedric Williamson, was the overeducated, under-used younger son of an earl. He had shunned the military and refused the Church, leaving himself few options to augment his quarterly allowance. He had a lively mind and too much time on his hands, a combination that made him a rollicking good companion for fun but perhaps a bit unreliable in a predicament, which is where he often found himself.

Alfred Collingwood shook his head slowly. "I think we m-might arrive a week too early for the h-hatching of the mayflies. The prime season b-begins in a fort-night."

Matt agreed. "I would prefer to wait until next week, myself." No need to say why, but every single day made him stronger. Seven more would be a big help.

Cedric drew a letter from his jacket. "Look here, in Perry's letter. He says he will expect us about the fifth."

Alfred took the letter from Cedric, unfolded it, and squinted at the handwriting. "So he does. About the f-fifth." He took a pinch of snuff and sneezed discreetly. "I can be ready to leave tomorrow. How about you, Matt?"

Matt hunted for a reason to postpone their departure in the lines of Perry's letter. "As he says, the hatching season is unpredictable, dependent on proper moisture and a few sunny days. Why should we rush to leave town so early?"

Cedric slapped his hand on the table, making their wine glasses jump. "Exactly because those demmed insects are unreliable. Give 'em one hot day and they might begin to pop."

"After our c-cold winter, don't the water have to warm up a little?"

Cedric waved Alfred's words away as if they were nothing at all. "The mayflies don't care about the cold. They reproduce regardless of temperature!"

"And how d-do you know that, old man?"

Matt could not help breaking into honest laughter. "Three grown men, arguing about the life cycle of mayflies. It begs comprehension!"

Alfred joined in the merriment. "I believe the creatures live less than t-twenty-four hours. Imagine cramming the essence of existence into s-such a brief period."

"But would you know the difference if you were a mayfly, Alfred?" Matt blotted an amused tear from the corner of his eye.

Cedric looked vexed. "It is not really the blasted fly we care about. It is the trout. They certainly know when those flies hatch."

Matt laughed even harder. "Of course it is the trout, Cedric. But the trout's behavior is entirely dependent on those insects. And that puts us in the same boat, scheduling our lives around the birth of baby mayflies."

"Well, it is demmed important, is it not? If we arrive after all the flies are eaten, the fish will not have any appetite and our competition will be ruined for another year. So I say, let us go tomorrow."

Alfred nodded in agreement. "I d-defer to the flies, the fish, and the carnal appetites of both. I will be ready tomorrow at whatever hour you say, Cedric, though I b-beg you to take pity on those such as I, who cannot rise before eleven."

Matt decided any further resistance would be futile. "If you all insist, I, too, shall be ready tomorrow."

Late in the afternoon, when Corey returned to Elaine's boudoir, she found her cousin sitting at the dressing table having her maid brush her long, dark hair.

"You seem to feel better, Elaine."

"Yes, a little. I slept for a while, then kept the toast down."

Corey stood beside her and their gaze met in the mirror. "I am glad to see you out of bed."

"I intend to go down for dinner. Perry likes me to

make the effort, even if I retire immediately afterwards."

"I understand." Corey looked at herself beside Elaine. Aside from her much lighter hair color, their faces had many features in common—the wide mouth, apple cheeks, and bright blue eyes. As children, they were often taken for twins instead of cousins, their close resemblance attributed to their common grandmother, the Countess of Aylmer. Though the girls knew her only as an elderly lady, she was one of those women about whom everyone said, *She was a celebrated beauty in her day.*

Elaine frowned at their reflection. "I see that we still look much alike, except that you have a tiny waist and your bosom does not sag. Compared to you, I look like a hag."

"Stop that nonsense, Elaine. You look lovely and just as you should, a contented countess with a fine family."

Elaine pushed her maid away and moved out of view of the mirror. "Yes, I know I should have not a complaint in the world. But you have not yet met the children."

She turned to the maid, who was straightening the brushes on the dressing table. "Please have Bess bring the children in. And tell her to be sure they are on their best behavior." Elaine turned to Corey and waved her to a seat. "Tell me of your parents. Are they well?"

"Oh, yes. But, Father is dreading the autumn when he must turn over his flock to another vicar."

"So he is not looking forward to a quiet retirement?"

"Not at all. Mother would like to go to Bath to live, take him away from watching the new man change things at All Saints Church to his own ways."

"I see her viewpoint."

"As do I, but it all depends on money. Bath would be ideal for both of them, but they still send every penny they can spare to my brother."

"Georgie is still not able to stand on his own?"

"We all hope he will soon find his calling, but it seems he suffers one disaster after another. None of his endeavors so far has yielded him a sufficient income."

"Would you go to Bath with your parents?"

Corey decided not to tell Elaine about her plan to find a position so she could help her mother and father. How could Elly, living in this palace, understand what it meant to have no money and very little hope to earn more than a pittance? "I do not know. I am mulling the alternatives." That was certainly true, she thought.

Even through the closed door, Corey could hear a piercing shriek from the corridor, followed by loud sobs.

Elaine's face grew grim, her lips tight. "That foolish Bess cannot handle Henry and Gina. She is an impossibly hopeless ninny."

The door opened and two tear-stained faces peeked around it, wailing, "Mama, Mama."

"Wipe your eyes immediately, Henry." The edge to Elaine's voice surprised Corey. "You should be ashamed at crying. You are four years of age! And we have a guest."

The child sniffled and rubbed at his nose. His lower lip stuck out and he frowned. "I am sorry, Mama."

"That is much better, Henry. And Gina, I expect you to wipe your eyes and stop that gruesome howling."

Gina plopped herself down on the carpet and continued to weep. The little girl's face was red, her cheeks stained with watery streaks. Her big blue eyes made Corey want to kiss the tears away.

Elaine sounded as though she was on the edge of a tantrum herself. "Bess, whatever have you been doing with them? What is going on in that nursery?"

Bess, an awkward girl of no more than seventeen, opened her mouth to speak, then seemed to change her mind. She stared at the floor.

Elaine's frown deepened. "Do something about that girl. I cannot abide that noise."

Bess took a step toward Gina, who looked up and sobbed louder, tearing the ribbon out of her hair and throwing it on the floor.

"Georgina!" Elaine looked as if she was about to cry herself.

Corey stepped over to the child and crouched beside her, smoothing her hair off her forehead. "Shh, dear. You will give Mama the headache."

Gina seemed surprised someone had come to her. She stopped crying for a few seconds, then continued but in a much quieter way.

Corey whispered to her. "Mama wants to see you smile, Gina."

Gina shook her head, tossing her curls back and forth. "No."

Corey realized that Elaine, Henry, and Bess were all staring at her, waiting for her to quiet Gina. Gina herself peered at Corey from under her drooping curls all the while she continued to sniffle.

Corey stood and extended her hand. "Come sit on my lap, Gina, and we will dry your eyes."

Corey took a chair near Elaine and held out the handkerchief Bess gave her. Slowly, still giving little sobs, much like those in which Elaine had indulged earlier, Gina edged closer until she sat at Corey's feet. Still looking skeptical, the little girl put up her arms.

Corey reached down and scooped her up, hugging her close. "Now, there, is that not better?"

Gina blew her nose on a corner of the hankie.

Elaine delicately touched her eyes with a lacy square. "You see, Corey? I knew you had a special touch with children."

Corey caressed Gina's silky curls. How could one not want to hug an adorable child like this?

"Be careful, Corey. You will get your dress all wet."

Indeed, Gina's tears had stained the front of Corey's simple pale blue gown. "I am sure it will dry. A few tears cannot hurt this muslin."

"I hope not." Elaine beckoned to Henry. Still wearing a glower, the boy inched over to his mama, who put her arm around him. "Henry, this is my cousin, Miss Bransford. Give her a proper bow."

Henry, still frowning, bent from the waist, a reasonable approximation of a bow.

"Now say, 'I am happy to make your acquaintance, cousin.'"

He mumbled the words without taking his eyes from the carpet.

Elaine looked about to reprimand the boy for a less-than-stellar performance.

Corey could not help grinning. "I am pleased to make your acquaintance, Lord Henry. I hope you will call me Corey."

"What do you say, Henry?" Elaine seemed determined to make the boy into a pattern card of respectability.

"Thank you, Corey." Henry raised his eyes, though he still looked hostile.

Corey cradled Gina in her arms. "And Gina, my dear, I am very happy to know you, too."

Blessedly, Elaine did not demand the child make a curtsy. "Now you may sit on the windowseat, Henry."

The boy followed directions while Bess edged into the corner, trying her best to look invisible.

Corey rocked a little in her chair, and felt Gina's breaths on her chest. The child was quieting at last. "I think we shall all have a lovely time this summer. I am looking forward to having you show me around, Henry. And Gina, if you have a doll, we might sew her a new dress." She could feel the child nodding her head.

Elaine gave a deep sigh. "You do know how much I appreciate your help, Cordelia. You are an angel. How I would cope with my condition, and with these wretched men arriving, I could not bear it without your help."

Corey rocked slowly. "What men are arriving?"

"Those old friends of Perry's, the ones they used to call the Quorn Quartet. You remember them, those despicable ruffians who . . . well, one hopes they have matured a bit."

Corey's heart thumped so hard she feared it would frighten Gina. "You do not mean Cedric Williamson and Lord Matthew Allerton? Please say they will not be here?" Of all the men in the entire realm, these were the two Corey least wanted to see, much less spend the summer with.

"Exactly. Cedric, Matt, and Alfred Collingwood. Certainly you remember . . ."

"Remember? How could I forget? Cedric almost proposed marriage to me. Luckily, I diverted him before he . . ."

"Of course! I had forgotten. Oh, Corey, I am sorry I forgot. I was so wrapped up in my betrothal to Perry then that I hardly paid any attention to your romance."

Corey could hardly catch her breath. "No, Elaine, it was not a romance, really. I think Cedric got carried away by Perry's happiness, but there was never a true romance."

Elaine brightened. "Then perhaps I should see if I could rekindle—"

"Good heavens, no! I could not bear it. Truthfully, I never liked Cedric much at all. He was far too silly and brash."

His friend Matt was quite another story. But Corey dared not let Elaine know that. She might get even more ideas in her head.

First, Elaine's pregnancy. Then, the children to care for. Now, meeting up with the Quorn Quartet again. Could anything more happen to ruin her idyllic summer?

Two

A young maid served Corey her morning chocolate in a dainty pot of rosy porcelain adorned with delicate gilt patterns. Neither the beauty of the china nor the warmth of the liquid did anything to relieve the cloud of impending doom Corey felt. She sat propped up on lacy pillows in an elegant canopied bed, more luxurious than any she had occupied for several years. But how could she look forward to the day when she faced two hurdles she dreaded? Two tasks she was quite incapable of handling. Two challenges for which she had no aptitude whatsoever.

Elaine expected Perry's three friends today or tomorrow. During the night, in the midst of her tossing and turning, Corey relived their rackety antics, their irresponsible nonsense, their imprudent foolishness. Since her one London Season, she had heard little of them, other than Elaine's letters about her Perry, the only one of the four to have married.

The summer was looking less and less like a pleasant one, more and more like penance for some unnamed sins. Of course she could go home and leave Elaine to fend for herself. But that was a heartless thing to do, not to mention the coward's way out.

Thoughts of Lord Matthew Allerton stirred Corey's memory, unwelcome thoughts she had long tried to

suppress. Amazing that those precious few recollections were so vividly impressed in her mind. Partner for
a few dances, presence at a few morning calls in which
he served primarily as a comrade for Cedric. One little
stolen kiss. But enough to fuel years of dreaming.

Corey never quite understood what had given
Cedric the right to call himself her suitor. Certainly
she had never encouraged him. In fact, she had downright discouraged him. But all that Season, it was as if
Cedric Williamson had circulated some special notice
among the gentlemen of the *ton* that Miss Cordelia
Bransford was his choice, set aside for him. No one
else was to have the opportunity to court her. It was as
though she was marked as reserved for Cedric.

She remembered wondering about it at the time,
though she had never thought her first Season would
also be her last, and had not been excessively concerned. Lord Matthew, anyway, was just as foolish and
immature in some of the exploits he carried out with
his friends. At times she had wondered how Elaine
could take Perry's offer seriously.

All of it had ended, though, once she went home to
Mitton Moorby to tend to her mother, made ill by the
dreadful news of Georgie's troubles. Troubles, ha!
George had been accused of cheating at cards, and in
view of his mountain of debts to friends, enemies,
and cent-percenters alike, no one believed he could
possibly be innocent. Not even his parents. Especially
his sister.

From that moment on, there had been no funds for
anything but paying off George's obligations and
financing his new start across the ocean.

From that moment on, Corey's dreams of making
an advantageous match faded, bit by bit, until today

she considered herself a confirmed spinster, quite permanently on the shelf.

Yet, often in the depth of night, she remembered that London Season, and the face that haunted her dreams was that of Lord Matthew Allerton.

She had such contradictory feelings about him, a strong dose of attraction yet misgivings about his prankster-ish side, which reminded her too much of Georgie. That was the side of Matthew that left her with a sour feeling and troubling ambiguities she could not overcome.

As if the situation with the children were not bad enough, her second hurdle for the day! Obviously, Elaine meant Corey to supervise Henry and Gina, supervision they clearly needed and did not get from either Bess or their mother.

What did she know of children? At least her childhood had been idyllic. How had her mother treated her, disciplined her? Corey could not remember being punished. Somehow her parents had instilled in her a sense of obedience and a desire to please them. How was she to do that with Henry and Gina?

Moreover, how did they occupy their day? Beyond reading to them, which she hoped to do someday, what kinds of things did they do? Corey tried to remember how she filled her childhood days. She had a doll. Balls. And puzzles.

As she stared out the window at the cloudy sky, a shaft of sunlight broke through, casting rays of gold over the distant oaks. There was an advantage to being with the children. If she spent time with them, she would not be around the men, called on to witness their silly contests.

Corey poured another cup of chocolate and sipped

slowly. The housekeeper spoke of taking the children to see their baby brother in the village. Those visits would take her well away from the fields of competition. As Mrs. Newsome said, Henry and Gina needed fresh air and outdoor exercise. And the maid, Maggie, would take care of the children in the afternoon.

Not two hours later, one of the grooms led a fat bay pony down the driveway. Behind it was a unique cart with tall woven sides, unlike any Corey had seen. It looked too top-heavy to negotiate the rutted lanes, but its high sides would keep the children secure.

"Bess, was that made specially for the children?"

"Yes, miss. Lord Lodesham don't want 'em fallin' out."

"A very clever idea. What do you call this equipage?"

Bess looked bewildered. "Why, I guess the basket cart, miss."

Corey helped the glowering Gina climb in, while scowling Henry shook off Bess's hand. Seated, Corey and Bess could see over the high sides, but Gina and Henry stood on the benches in order to look out. Once they were aboard, the groom led the pony away from the house and turned into a lane leading to the village of Lodesham.

Out of the corner of her eye, Corey saw Henry give Gina a push, which violence she returned with a punch to his arm. He reached over and yanked a strand of her hair.

"He pulled my hair!" Gina's cries were piercing.

Corey looked at Bess, who said nothing. Frustrated, Corey moved over between the two children. "There, there, Gina," she whispered in the girl's ear. "Do not let him see he can make you cry."

Gina only sobbed harder and moved away from Corey toward the back of the cart.

Corey turned to the boy. "Henry, pulling hair is not allowed. Would you like to have your hair pulled?"

"I would not care." He gave her a surly look, as if defying her authority.

"We are going to see your baby brother and I expect you both to behave." Corey found her handkerchief and reached over to dry Gina's tears. The child pushed her away.

"Gina, please wipe your nose, dear." Gina took the handkerchief and rubbed it across her face ineffectually. Corey gave her a smile, but did not try to remedy the situation.

The children were more of a handful than Corey had imagined. She was surprised to find she had no idea how to gain their confidence and esteem. "Has it been a long time since you saw your baby brother?"

"Mama took us last time. It was cold."

"What do you call that pony?"

"Tommy. He is getting old. Papa has promised me my very own pony for my next birthday. I want a black one and I will call him Midnight."

Gina pursed her lips and nodded. "So do I. A black pony."

"You don't get one until you are five, Gina, just like me."

Corey felt a pang of remembrance. Long ago she had been just like Gina, full of defiance as she challenged her older brother. Best to stop this before it got very far. "Black is an excellent color for a pony. Though I am partial to dapple gray myself."

Henry's attention was diverted. "Why gray?"

"I like the silvery quality of the color. Especially in the mane and tail, like moonlight."

Gina almost mumbled to herself. "I want a silver pony named Moonlight."

Henry ignored her. "Papa's favorite horse is a chestnut called Flyer because he runs as fast as a bird flies. Papa says he will win lots of races."

Corey kept the children talking as they crossed a stone bridge over a stream and entered the village. An inn and half a dozen houses clustered around the green in front of the church. Down a side lane, she could hear the clang of a smith's hammer. Otherwise the hamlet was quiet until two boys ran up to the pony cart and called out to Henry. They were dressed in loose shirts with old trousers rolled up above their sturdy footwear, in sharp contrast to Henry's tan pantaloons and matching jacket with a wide lace collar and shiny, buckled shoes.

The boys' excitement showed in their dance beside the cart. "We got pups. They come last week."

Gina broke into a full smile, her eyes shining. "Puppies. I wanna see the puppies."

Bess had to grab Henry to keep him from trying to climb out.

In moments they stopped at a little garden in front of a cottage. The boys had run ahead to alert Mrs. Hitchens, who stood near the door, a chubby baby squirming in her arms. She wore a clean but shapeless gown in no particular style. Corey was glad to see she looked like the kind of woman who might answer a few questions about tending children. Henry ran to her for a hug.

"Good morning, Mrs. Hitchens." Corey helped Gina climb out of the basket trap. "I am Miss Brans-

ford, Lady Lodesham's cousin. I brought Lord Henry
and Lady Georgina to see their brother."

Mrs. Hitchens curtsied, as much as she could with
an armload of baby, and smiled shyly. Gina reached up
to touch the baby's dress, and Mrs. Hitchens set him
on the grass. Gina kissed him and made a funny face,
which made him laugh.

Mrs. Hitchens spoke softly. "He be a 'appy child."

Corey crouched down and reached out a hand. He
grabbed her finger and tried to pull it to his mouth.
Corey could not help laughing.

Mrs. Hitchens scooped him up again while Henry
and Gina scampered off with the two boys, both of
whom where chattering about new puppies down the
lane.

"Will they be all right?"

Mrs. Hitchens turned to a young girl of nine or ten
standing in the door. "Go along with 'em, Nell. They
jes' wanna see the new pups. Can I git ye a cup of tea,
miss?"

"Yes, thank you. That would be very nice."

Corey followed the woman inside and sat where directed at a scrubbed wooden table.

The tea was weak but the slice of freshly baked
bread was delicious, adorned with rich butter and
gooseberry jam. Corey watched Mrs. Hitchens bounce
baby Lawrence on her lap and make him laugh.
"Lawrence looks like a healthy little lad."

"He be a sturdy one, all right. And soon 'll be walkin',
I expect."

"He is adorable." Corey wanted to ask when he'd be
returned to his mama, but held her tongue. She had
no idea what kind of arrangements Elaine had with
Mrs. Hitchens.

"M'lady don't visit 'im much. I hear she's feelin' poorly."

Corey winced. Was Elaine's condition known here? If this village was like her own, everyone would have known of the countess's pregnancy as soon as her maid suspected. Corey contented herself with a smile and a shrug. "Yes, from time to time she is less than well."

Mrs. Hitchens's baby crawled to Corey and turned up her cherubic face, babbling in her own unique tongue.

"'Ow Tilly, you leave the nice lady be."

"Oh, she is fine. May I hold her?"

"If'n ye want."

Corey reached down and raised the child to her lap, surprised at the weight of her. Like Henry and Gina, she had a mop of fair golden hair curling onto her chubby cheeks. "How old is she, Mrs. Hitchens?"

"Two months over a year now."

Corey looked around the small cottage, probably two rooms upstairs and one large room down. A big iron pot hung in the large hearth and the smell of stewing meat competed with the scent of bread fresh from the oven.

"How many children do you have, Mrs. Hitchens?"

"Nell's the oldest, then Teddy, Benjamin, Sukey, and the baby."

Corey decided the best approach was to watch and learn. Here was a woman who obviously dealt with several children at the same time, from the infant at her breast to another young girl checking the oven. Over breakfast that morning, Corey had learned from Mrs. Newsome about the wet nurse, and other tenants of the earl who lived in the village. Mr. Hitchens worked as one of the estate gardeners, the one who had the greatest talent for the roses.

Mrs. Hitchens's children curtsied and minded their manners. Corey already saw her calmness and patience. Common sense said that was the way to make children behave, not tears, not sharp demands, not yielding to their every whim. Corey might have no experience with children, but she felt certain neither Elaine nor Bess would do as a model on which to base her efforts.

When Corey asked her more about her family, Mrs. Hitchens's sun-lined face crinkled with a shy smile.

"The boys, they be gettin' a bit o' work in the summer hayin' an' weedin' the vegetables. Me Arthur won't let 'em near them roses. Too precious for unskilled hands, Arthur says, he does."

"Lady Lodesham is very fond of her roses. She has written to me about them many times."

"It be sumthin' to see an' sniff when they be in bloom."

"I am looking forward to it."

Corey roused herself from the peaceful setting. They should head back home before Elaine, or more likely Mrs. Newsome, began to worry. She could have stayed here all day in this pleasant little house. In fact, she expected she would often seek refuge here once those men arrived.

The thought of the Quorn Quartet brought a frown to her forehead. Back during her London Season when Perry was courting Elaine, she and her cousin at first were amused by the antics of the four close friends, energetic young men whose escapades provided many a laugh. One scrape after another, one reckless feat on top of another silly prank. But after two months, their antics looked lame and their jokes pitiful. Corey had needed no judicious advice from high sticklers to discourage Cedric Williamson's feeble attempts at courting her.

The church bell was just chiming the noon hour when Corey finally got the children settled in the basket cart. She held Gina in her arms and Henry sat next to her with Bess, who had hardly uttered a word all morning on the other seat. The groom led the pony away from Mrs. Hitchens's house back toward the village green.

Corey knew she would come back often, not only to hide from the quartet. Mrs. Hitchens's house was modest, but more comfortable in its modesty than the elegant Hall with its hordes of servants and unhappy mistress. All of Mrs. Hitchens's children were well behaved, sweet and dear, but the babies, well, the babies were special. Holding them almost made Corey want to weep. The way things were going in her life, she would never have one of these precious bundles of her own. That thought was especially painful when her arms were full, her gaze met a pair of big blue eyes, and her ears were filled with gurgles of infant laughter.

In her heart she could almost hear the coos of her own babies. The sharp bite of tears stung her eyes, and her throat filled with a throbbing ache.

Corey swiped at her damp eyes with the back of her hand. Before she daydreamed herself into sobs, she'd better put such pathetic twaddle out of her head. She forced herself to listen to Gina's babbling about the pups.

"Two are brown and two mixed-up."

"All hounds are spotted, you widgeon." Henry's voice

carried a note of superiority, as the elder brother who had much more experience. Corey felt another pang of recollection, another jolt of emotional turmoil.

Gina made a face and stuck out her tongue at her brother. "I am not a widgeon. You are a nodcock!"

"Enough!" Corey spoke with what she hoped was a tone of authority the children would obey.

Henry aimed a sour look at her that might have withered the roses from the vines. Gina, enjoying the last word in their tiff, set her jaw proudly.

The cart bumped gently over the ruts of the lane, rocking and jostling Henry against her while she held Gina on her other side. They rounded the corner of the churchyard, passed several cottages, and reached the edge of the village green. The peaceful scene was broken by shouts of deep-throated laughter.

Across the stretch of grass stood a small coaching inn. In front of it were three men dressed in handsome breeches and coats of bottle green. Though they were a bit too far away for her to make out their faces, Corey knew them: the three expected at Lodesham Hall. Cedric Williamson, Alfred Collingwood, and Lord Matthew Allerton joined with Perry, Lord Lodesham, to make up their self-proclaimed Quorn Quartet.

The three men held tankards of ale and seemed to be singing, or attempting to sing. Corey was relieved the breeze carried the words away from her, for it was sure to be a bawdy tune, by the broad grins on their faces. Was that not just like them, to be engaged in some ridiculous and worthless claptrap!

As the distance narrowed, she made out Lord Matthew Allerton's delicious grin, the way a lock of his dark hair strayed onto his forehead. He dressed impeccably, as did the other two. These men probably cared as much about their raiment as any lady she ever knew, perhaps more. The cut of a jacket, the precise number of fobs, the size of their jacket buttons. Yet they dressed soberly in comparison to the London dandies. Lord Matthew wore his buff breeches and dark green coat, almost a uniform for his Corinthian set, with style and grace, an élan that set him apart. At least to her eyes.

Not very smart, Cordelia, she warned herself. *If you are not to suffer a great disappointment, you must gird yourself for possibly being spurned by him.* Five years ago, she knew she had the freshness of youth, the wide-eyed artlessness and purity that sometimes captivated men, at least for a short time. Now, she felt like she was only a bony, angular ape-leader, her once-pretty golden hair a dullish color, pulled back into a tight bun.

She was bereft of sparkling conversation as well. She knew nothing of the London scene in which these gentlemen were so at home. No clever *on dits* would spring to her lips, nothing like what these town-smart blades were used to with the bejeweled and groomed beauties of the city. She would be, to them, exactly what she was to herself, a rather drab and boring country mouse. Unworthy of their interest. Ineligible for their attention.

As the basket cart proceeded toward the other side of the green, a goose girl appeared at the widest end, driving a flock of geese to graze in the long grass. She was no more than ten, and wore a blue apron and a cotton bonnet.

When the men spotted her, one of them whooped with joy. Corey wrinkled her nose in distaste.

"Three guineas that far goose beats the others to the end of the green!"

Another chimed in. "That third one will win."

If any of the three men bothered that little goose girl, Corey intended to climb out of the cart and confront them. For the moment, however, she much preferred to be at a distance, unknown to them, her face, like the girl's, obscured by her bonnet. There would be more than enough time to see those three coxcombs at the Hall. For now, let them carouse their childish way here in the village.

As the cart moved closer, Corey watched the three men slap coins on the table in front of the inn and settle down in chairs to watch the geese. What silly fellows, still acting like schoolboys. Betting on geese! How very foolish.

Not a very exciting match, Corey mused, as the geese were unhurried, weaving back and forth in search of whatever it was they found to their liking.

One of the men stood again. "They are too slow!"

Corey could see now that the speaker was none other than her former suitor, Cedric Williamson. He was handsome as ever, five years having changed not a feature on his face. Nor, she noted, had Alfred Collingwood changed, unless it might be his forehead was a bit higher from a slight loss of hair. Served him right. Too bad he had not developed a bald spot. Lord Matthew Allerton's face was darkened by the sun and as he moved he seemed to favor one leg, almost limping. Probably fell off his horse in a drunken stupor.

Corey prepared to jump out of the cart as Collingwood approached the goose girl. But she waited a moment. He seemed to be asking the girl to use her

switch to encourage the geese to hurry their meandering way across the green. She shook her head shyly,
keeping her face toward the ground. Collingwood
reached in his pocket for a coin, but she continued to
shake her head. Shrugging, he called to the others.
"No d-dice. She cannot be bribed."

Corey sat back. Her intervention was not needed.

Alfred's shouts caused a couple of the geese to hop
away from him, spreading their wings and squawking.

"Confound it, Al. Look what you have done." Cedric
shook his fist. "Now they are all mixed up. Don't know
which one is mine."

Corey giggled to herself. The white geese were
identical, at least to her eyes. Perhaps their mothers
would have known them, but if there was any difference in them from a few feet away, she could not
imagine what it was.

Obviously, the three men had not changed much
since she knew them in London five years ago. And if
their antics today foretold anything about their behavior once they got to the Hall, Elaine was exactly
right in dreading their stay.

Mr. Collingwood tried to chase the geese, but they
merely fluttered out of his way, quickly turning back
to graze again, some of them even reversing direction
and moving off to the side or back in the direction of
the widest end of the green. Corey found the goose
girl's reaction amusing, a little smile on her nearly
shadowed face as the grown man jumped about, waving his arms just as small boys were wont to do in the
midst of a flock, whether ducks, chickens, or geese.
Again he tried to shoo one, and suddenly the goose
turned and hissed at him, spreading its wings and
waggling its head with menace.

Collingwood backed quickly away, causing his two companions to hoot in derision.

"Alfred, you looby! Running from a goose!"

In Corey's arms, Gina had drifted into sleep, her long, pale eyelashes against her milky white cheeks. Henry watched the men with interest, no doubt wishing he could chase the geese as well. Corey gave a mental shrug. Obviously the men were as bad as they had ever been. Next thing you knew, they probably would be trying to scale the church steeple to ring the bell in the middle of the night or toss mud balls at someone's laundry hung out to dry.

The men hardly looked in her direction. They showed not the slightest interest in the basket cart or the groom, thankfully not in the Lodesham livery, leading the pony.

Corey did not wish to be recognized. Nor did she wish to engage in conversation with any of these scoundrels. She knew she could not keep her disdain for their nonsensical behavior out of her voice. Anyway, there was more than enough time for her to speak with all of them, probably beginning before dinner this very evening. Clearly they would not stay at this rural inn when the sumptuous accommodations of the Hall were a five-minute ride away. No, this was just a last stop on their way to partake of the lavish hospitality of the Earl of Lodesham and his countess.

Henry watched the geese as the cart moved toward the lane leading to the Hall. "Why is that man chasing the geese?"

"Because he is being silly."

The boy thought about that for a moment before nodding. "Yes, that is silly. I chased a duck once but I

never caught it. It jumped into the pond and all I got
were muddy shoes. Our old nurse was very angry."

Someday, Corey thought, when everyone else was
far away, she would let the boy take off his shoes and
stockings and walk in the mud, letting it squeeze between his toes. Every child, regardless of the sober
mien of his nurse, should know what it felt to splash
in puddles and run barefoot through the warm summer grass, away from the scrutiny of a paid attendant
more concerned about cleaning up after the child
than his adventurous spirit.

She looked back toward the green but they had
turned a corner and neither the men nor the geese
were in view. Perhaps the behavior of those three men
would be different today if they had been able to
chase butterflies or catch tadpoles as little boys. Had
their proper families ever allowed them to run free
and enjoy childhood?

Maggie was waiting for them when the basket cart
approached the Hall. The maid gathered Gina into
her arms, clucking at the child's mussed dress and
snarled hair, muttering under her breath. "Your
mama will not be happy to see you looking so messy,
my girl. And Henry, you look like you have been running too much. Your face is red, your shoes are all
scuffed, and your stockings fallen down."

Corey knew the maid and Bess were only trying to do
their jobs. Nevertheless, she was not in a mood to let
them chastise Henry or Gina. "Maggie, the children
were merely playing."

"Not with Mrs. Hitchens's children, I hope. That is
not allowed, you know, miss."

"No, I did not know they were not to play."

"The rules may be different when they are with you,

miss, but when they are with me, they are not allowed to associate with children in the village. Bad influences, of all kinds."

As bad as watching a grown man try to chase a goose? Corey wanted to ask. But she merely smiled and nodded as Maggie and Bess bustled away with her charges.

As she climbed out of the cart, Corey looked down at her own dress, rumpled and creased.

"Thank you, Jem," she said.

The groom turned and touched his forehead in the traditional indication of respect before he led the pony and cart toward the stable.

Corey hurried into the house. The three men might not be far behind them, unless their wagers were taking longer than usual. Or if they decided to have another tankard, which was very likely. Nevertheless she decided to check on Elaine and then spend the rest of the afternoon finishing the trim on her newest gown, the one she planned to wear at the first dinner she shared with the Quorn Quartet. She did not consider herself a vain person, but she did not want them to think of her as a dowd, either.

Three

Matt tossed down the last of his ale and set the tankard on the table. He gave a handful of coins to the innkeeper. "You will no doubt see more of us here at the Red Lion the next weeks."

The man's ruddy face crinkled in a broad smile. "Yes, m'lord, that would please me mightily. Indeed it would."

Matt stood and clapped him on the shoulder. "I'm going for my rig."

Alfred tipped his tankard with a satisfied smack. "That last one was entirely s-superfluous, but doubly delicious. Matt, we'll be right with you." He heaved himself to his feet and nudged Cedric, who slept where he sat at the table, his head resting on his folded arms.

"What?" Cedric blinked and groaned aloud.

Matt walked into the coachyard, carefully suppressing his urge to favor the sore leg. When out of his friends' sight, he allowed himself to wince at the stiffness he felt. Perhaps he should have been up chasing those geese with Al instead of sitting for over an hour.

A young boy held his pair, watered and rested, ready for the last, short stage of their journey to Perry's country seat. He hoisted himself into the curricle and took up the reins. Alfred's and Cedric's saddle horses needed only to have their girths tightened to be ready whenever their riders managed to separate themselves from the local brew. Matt nodded to the groom to release the horses and headed the pair out of the yard.

A quarter-hour later, Matt watched the Lodesham grooms unharness the pair. He leaned against the stable door, kneading his thigh as if he could rub away the ache. When Alfred and Cedric rode up, calling their hellos, Matt crossed his arms over his chest and adopted a casual stance.

As his friends dismounted, he strolled over to hold the bridle of Alfred's rangy chestnut.

Alfred brushed the dust from his shoulders. "I have been m-meaning to ask you, Matt. How come you did not bring a saddle horse?"

Matt gave a nonchalant shrug. "Zeus will arrive tomorrow, coming with my man and the baggage. I decided the new grays needed the workout." He handed Alfred's horse to a groom.

Alfred applied his handkerchief to his boots. "I see. Ah, here is P-Perry."

Matt turned to see the fourth member of the quartet, their host, striding toward them.

They shouted and laughed and slapped each other's backs, exchanging greetings enthusiastically. Once the greetings were out of the way, Perry and Cedric broke into some playful sparring, dancing around each other, then reaching out to cuff Matt. The punch took him by surprise, throwing him off balance. He made a quick recovery and threw his own light punches, but in moments the strain threatened his leg.

"Whoa there, watch my casting arm. I have a lot of fish to catch, Cedric." But no one paid attention to his jest.

Alfred darted into the fray and like a gaggle of schoolboys, all four were soon rolling on the ground, wrestling and laughing, heaving deep breaths, panting, all in good fun.

When they had all had enough, they stood, brushed each other off, and headed for the house. Halfway there, Perry slapped Matt on the back, simply the last straw for Matt's bad leg. It bent beneath him and only Perry's strong grab for his arm kept Matt on his feet.

"Say, there, Matt. I thought that leg was all healed."

Matt tried to laugh the concern away. "Was, until I took up again with you ruffians." He forced his leg to bear his weight and they proceeded.

"By gad, man, you are limping. Thought you was all recovered."

Perry looked Matt straight in the eye. "Come clean, Matt. Are you? Fully recovered, I mean."

Matt used his heartiest voice. "Of course. Could not be better."

Cedric looked from Matt to Perry. "Are you sure?"

Alfred set his hands on his hips. "Is that why you d-drove instead of rode?"

"You three cackle like a henhouse full of pullets. If I was not looking at the Quorn Quartet, I would have sworn I wandered into an ancient bunch of valetudinarians swathed in blankets sitting in their Bath chairs."

Perry appeared unconvinced. "Well, if you have any residual problems with that old wound, we don't have to indulge in foot races or anything else that puts you at a disadvantage."

Matt summoned a jovial laugh. "If I had to use a crutch I would not be at any disadvantage with the likes of you dithering old crones. Put your mind at ease, Perry. I intend to leave all of you in my dust."

As they covered the rest of the distance, Matt suspected he had not heard the last of Perry's worry. Somehow, Matt had to be sure those fears were crushed. If he had wanted to be treated as an invalid, he could have stayed at his brother's, where he had been for eight months after he left the hospital. Between the duchess and his mother, the dowager duchess, he had been entirely suffocated.

Elaine held out her arm for Corey to fasten a diamond bracelet around her wrist. "You know, I assume, the three men have arrived?"

Corey nodded as she fastened the clasp. "Fanny told me when she helped with my hair."

"You look very nice, Corey."

"Thank you. I hope I will not embarrass you." Corey knew she would be a smudge on the lovely surface of the Lodesham Hall scene this evening. Not only was her ensemble too simple, but the prospect of the dinner ahead made her head ache. She hoped to endure the evening without snapping at anyone or otherwise losing her composure.

Elaine began to wring her hands, the diamonds flashing in the candlelight. "Perry is the one who should be embarrassed at foisting those fellows on our company. I cannot think what possessed him to reinstate this childish competition of theirs."

"Competition? What do you mean?"

"Perry says they used to meet every spring to hold a fishing contest. Lodesham Hall's stretch of the river is famous for trout, you know."

"You mean those three men came to fish?" An activity requiring such patience seemed ill-suited to the dispositions of the trio Corey watched on the village green earlier in the day.

"They started this when they were boys. They called themselves the Quorn Quartet because they became friends when they hunted with their fathers in Leicestershire. They aspired to be Corinthians of the first stare, Perry said."

"Whatever that term means. My brother always said he was a Corinthian. But to me, he was a spendthrift and a very bad gambler."

Elaine nodded. "Appallingly bad, indeed he was. But Perry is proud to be called a Corinthian. He says Corinthians are gentlemen who excel in sporting endeavors, compete fairly, and respect the highest ideals of honor and loyalty."

Again, Corey thought about the scene in the village earlier, but resisted telling Elaine. Nothing about chasing geese on the green would comfort her cousin.

Elaine went on, her voice growing more disparaging. "Year after year they fished together in the spring. Perry says they also competed at archery and fencing, sometimes raced their horses, even held footraces. All they thought about was besting one another."

"But apparently the challenges built a bond among them?"

"Exactly. Until they kidnapped Perry from our honeymoon."

"You wrote only a little bit about that, Elly. They actually took him away, physically?"

"The wedding was here at the Hall. We went to a neighboring estate for our first few days together. But those dreadful fellows came the next morning and spirited Perry away before he knew what was going on."

"What did you do?"

"Oh, Corey, I was hysterical. They left me a note saying they would return him soon, but it was not until the next day they brought him back."

"You mean they kept him all night?"

"Yes. I was ready to dispatch a servant to tell the family he had been abducted. Matt and Cedric and Alfred all thought it was a great lark, and even Perry laughed about it until he realized how distraught I was."

Corey shook her head in astonishment. "I can hardly believe they would do such a thing to their friend."

"Perry cut off the connection, to spare my feelings. But last winter when he proposed inviting them again, I agreed. There must have been something wrong with my feeble brainbox. Now I count on you, Corey, to help me through the ordeal."

"I will do my best, but I am not particularly fond of any of them. Other than Perry, that is."

At last Elaine smiled. "Perry's mama says that marriage has matured him. Although that is the nicest statement she has ever made about me."

"The dowager countess must have been delighted to have an heir for Perry."

"She considered it quite unseemly, coming too soon, just nine months after the wedding. Then when Gina arrived only one year later . . . the dowager Lady Lodesham did not approve then, nor of Lawrence's arrival. Now, there will be another. She will be livid."

Corey shook her head in disbelief. "Certainly you are being oversensitive, Elly. I thought all mothers loved becoming grandmothers."

"Ha! You have not met the dragon dowager. Thank

heavens Lodesham Hall has no dower house. With my earnest blessing, Perry gave her one of his small properties in Kent."

"Does Perry not have brothers or sisters?"

Elaine walked to the mirror and inspected her image. "Only a sister, Sophronia. I cannot imagine Lady Lodesham allowed the earl in her bed more than twice. No wonder he died so young."

Corey met her cousin's gaze in the mirror and they both broke into giggles.

Corey stood beside Elaine and bit back her laughter. "At least we do not have to worry about her. I assume she is in London for the Season."

"Thank heavens, she is."

Corey had no desire to discuss the London Season. Her one year had not endeared her to its proceedings. "You look lovely, Elly."

Elaine drew a deep breath. "I feel a little better. I have asked for sherry to be served before dinner and perhaps I will have a small glass." Elaine turned sideways and smoothed her dress over her abdomen. "I do not believe I show yet. Do you agree?"

"Not a hint."

"Good. I hope Perry has not told those men we are to have another child so soon. Even without the dowager countess's disapproval, I find it embarrassing, besides a matter of considerable discomfort. And if those dreadful fellows leer at me with knowing grins . . ."

Corey handed Elaine her gloves and took her arm. "Come along, Elly. Let us face the foe with courage!"

Corey's concern for Elaine masked her own dread of the upcoming meeting. As they went downstairs, the thought of standing for a half-hour trying to talk with those three blades gave Corey a stomachache, hardly conducive to enjoying the art of the Lodesham chef.

At the door, four sets of eyes turned to them and a chorus of polite greetings rang out. You would almost believe them to be proper gentlemen, Corey thought. All were elegantly turned out in evening dress, and stood tall in the distinguished way of polite society. The Ivory Saloon, which last night had appeared so vast and stately, seemed almost crowded with the men. Even Perry's voice was louder. "My dear, and Miss Bransford, come in, come in."

"Countess!"

"Lady L-Lodesham!"

"How very lovely you look tonight."

The three guests outdid one another in their greetings to Elaine, one lifting her gloved hand and kissing the air just above her diamond-clad wrist, another bowing deeply and sweeping his hand forward, the third clasping his hand to his heart and declaring her an angel.

In a moment, Elaine waved them away. "I am sure you remember my cousin, Miss Bransford."

All three bowed, made themselves her servants in the most florid style.

"Miss Bransford, it is indeed a pleasure seeing you again."

"I am delighted to be in your delightful company once more."

"You are as l-lovely as ever, Miss Bransford. What brings you to Dorset?"

She felt surrounded, almost smothered, by their charming if insincere compliments. Corey ignored the magnificence of their praise, being clad in a simple gown with no jewelry, and being several years past the height of her youthful allure.

Captain Lord Matthew Allerton, faultlessly attired and still sporting his characteristic sly smile, as if he knew a secret no one else guessed. She hoped she never gave away the power he had to captivate her by nothing more than the hint of a smile or the arch of an eyebrow. She tried to suppress any reaction beyond the mildest acknowledgement of his presence.

Alfred Collingwood, wiry and dark, on the surface polite to a fault, but secretly, she guessed, at the helm of many of the group's romps. He affected a little stutter, and seemed constantly to play with an enameled snuff box.

Cedric Williamson, the man she might have married, if she had allowed him to finish his proposal. The most handsome of the three, with wavy, tousled hair that no doubt tempted the roving fingers of numerous ladies, most of dubious virtue.

And Peregrine, Lord Lodesham, gazing with fondness into the sparkling eyes of his wife, Elaine. She was a lucky lady, Corey thought, even though the babies came too frequently.

They escorted Corey to one of a pair of sofas, settling Elaine on the opposite one. Perry sat beside his wife with Lord Matthew on her other side. Mr. Collingwood and Cedric, Mr. Williamson, flanked Corey.

The butler stood sentinel over two footmen who handed around crystal glasses of sherry, then withdrew to the doorway where they stood at attention as if expecting an immediate summons to present arms in a military review.

"Thank you, Oakley." Perry dismissed the butler, who took his place beside the footmen.

Lord Matthew smiled in Corey's direction. "Miss Bransford, I believe it has been three or four Seasons since I danced with you at Lady Hipsley's ball."

Corey hoped she did not blush. "Five since I was in London, but do not try to convince me you actually remember that evening, Lord Matthew."

"Certainly I do. Cedric here stole you right away from me when I went to fetch refreshments."

Mr. Williamson bristled with exaggerated umbrage. "I say, Matt, I was only claiming my promised set. It was not to be taken lightly to have met Miss Bransford's approbation. One of that Season's most sought-after partners, she was."

Corey made the expected protest. "I was nothing of the kind."

Mr. Collingwood added his voice to the flirtatious banter. "You honored me only t-twice in all the evenings I suffered through Almack's simply to enjoy the c-company of you and Lady Lodesham."

Corey knew if she kept a smile on her face and looked interested, their chatter would continue. She stole a glance at Lord Matthew. Even long ago, when Cedric was her most persistent suitor, she had favored Lord Matthew. His countenance was less smooth and refined than Cedric's or Alfred's. His face, his entire bearing, had a more rugged look, yet he was the most polished of gentlemen on the surface. But she always scorned her tinge of attraction to Matt, attributing those feelings to a schoolgirl's penchant for the unattainable. He was the Oxford-educated son of a duke—a second son, to be sure. But she was the daughter of a vicar, only the granddaughter of an earl on her mother's side.

When they rose to go into dinner, Lord Matthew

out-jostled Cedric to take Corey's arm. "My turn. I will show you who has a long and accurate memory! Out of our way, knave!"

Grinning, Cedric backed away and made a sweeping gesture in the direction of the doorway.

Lord Matthew bowed to Corey. As the others moved to the dining room, he leaned close to her and whispered, "As a matter of fact, I have another memory you might recall as well. I particularly remember our little stroll in the moonlight that night at Lady Hipsley's."

His breath tickled her ear and she suppressed a shiver. Nevertheless, Corey felt a tingle run down her back as she matched her tone to his. "Come now, Lord Matthew. You remember no such thing. We merely stood on the balcony, for not more than a minute."

He continued in a low and husky voice. "In my memory, it was a much more protracted encounter. You were glowing in the moonlight in your white gown."

This time she could not suppress the tremor, or more precisely, the earthquake in the center of her being. Luckily, there was no time to reply before he held her chair and she sat down at the table.

Visions of that evening rumbled through her brain while she held herself rigid and hoped a flush did not color her cheeks. She balled her hands into fists to prevent them from shaking, and kept her eyes lowered to prevent meeting Lord Matthew's gaze, which seemed to burn into her. How dare he bring up that one small encounter? How dare he tease her by making it into something of significance? To Lord Matthew, it would have been the tamest moment in his vast experience with females. He certainly recalled it only because of his rivalry with Cedric, who had probably confessed his interest in her. The cad!

Corey wished she did not remember the evening quite so well. Lord Matthew had pressed shockingly close to her, and just as tonight, he whispered in her ear. But instead of seating her for dinner, he had placed a little kiss on her forehead. Surely he would have no memory of that. For him, it would have been nothing. For her, the kiss had been divine.

She shook off the reminiscence. Many years had passed and she had changed, even if Lord Matthew was still as much a jackanape as his fellow Quorn Quartet members.

Corey turned her attention to Elaine, who lifted a morsel of meat to her lips. She seemed to be surviving this trying dinner with minimal discomfort. Corey wished she could say the same for herself.

Cedric had been directing a number of remarks in her direction, and she had no idea what they were. She simply had to stop thinking of him as Cedric and refer to him in both her thoughts and her speech as Mr. Williamson. Though that form of address was much too dignified for such a scapegrace as he was, she needed to maintain the distance of some formality.

"Mr. Williamson, I understand you will be demonstrating your fly fishing expertise in the next few days. I had no idea your talents extended to angling."

"Aha! I will be delighted to show you how adept I am. But you are ignoring my questions, Cordelia."

"Please forgive me, Mr. Williamson. I fear I was not listening."

Mr. Collingwood gave a bark of laughter. "Take that, Cedric! The l-lady did not hear your enchanting words. Seems your usual romantic b-brilliance is losing its luster. A sad thing, indeed."

Corey nearly gasped in surprise at the quick, dark frown on Cedric's face before he managed a tight grin.

"Alfred, your powers of observation are even more feeble than usual."

Lord Lodesham called for their attention. "My dear wife wishes to know if you find your accommodations satisfactory."

Quickly the men competed to list the countless ways in which their bedchambers exceeded their every desire. Corey drew a deep breath. She hoped Cedric and Alfred would forget their little tiff.

When the extravagant compliments appeared to be winding down, Corey attempted to send the talk in a different, and perhaps lengthy, direction. "I understand you four used to meet here almost every spring."

Lord Matthew started to speak, but Cedric cut him off. "We have been after Perry's fish since we were lads . . ."

Corey settled back in her chair and nodded, and took a taste of the buttered crab. Before Cedric completed his remarks, Alfred interrupted him, followed by more explanations by Lord Matthew and Perry.

Before long, the four began to recount their youthful pranks, almost forgetting the presence of the ladies. Uncovering each detail brought a new round of laughter. Corey finished four tender stalks of asparagus dressed with lemon sauce.

"Remember the t-time we tricked the watchman into chasing us around the square and then we ran in different d-directions and he did not know which of us to follow?"

"Yes, yes. He was one confused fellow. Old fool."

Corey put a dab of turbot in her mouth to prevent yielding to the temptations of telling Mr. Collingwood just what she thought. How could healthy young men tease those old watchmen? Four against one, and the vagabonds were probably less than half his age. Could they be proud of such a caper?

Cedric was off on a new story. "Then there was the time we climbed the t-tower of that church and rang the bell. What a commotion that caused."

"Had the whole neighborhood thinking Napoleon's army was just one street away."

Corey sampled the duck. Better to chew than give vent to her irritation.

"And the time we brought the donkey into Lady Knott's drawing room after we tricked her into inviting Mr. Gray Longears? She was livid."

"And then we c-could not get him back down again until he had ruined her rugs."

"My father never forgot that one," Perry said. "He had to buy her a new Aubusson."

Corey's face felt like it would crack under the strain of maintaining an amiable expression. She kept her attention on the creamed peas.

"Oh, we were terrible. I remember hiding along the r-river and cutting loose all the wherrymen's boats one night. For that we were never caught."

"And what we did with that nightsoil collector's load! Remember that?"

Lord Matthew held up a hand. "Not at table, Cedric. Spare the lovely ears of these very compassionate and understanding ladies. Save that story for later."

Corey threw him a look of relief. Merciful heavens, the juvenile nature of their pranks was unfathomable. She nibbled another piece of the turbot.

Corey did not dare to meet Elaine's eyes. She was

sure Elaine was also trying to ignore this repugnant recital.

Not that any of the four would care what she thought of them. They had been raised in privilege to do nothing of use to society, perhaps encouraged by indulgent parents. Who could wonder they often went beyond mischief to outright vandalism?

At last, Elaine rose and wished the men a good night. Corey murmured similar words and followed Elaine from the dining room. All four men stood and bowed, as though they had made polite conversation all through the meal.

When she reached her boudoir, Elaine almost collapsed onto a sofa.

Corey perched beside her. "Are you not well, Elaine? Should I ring for your maid?"

"In a minute. Ah, Corey, how shall we survive the next few weeks? I declare, even Perry sounds childish when the Quartet gets talking. I find it sadly lowering. My husband speaks like a silly boy!"

"Do not be too hard on Perry, my dear Elly."

"They did dreadful things. Did they also steal coins from bent old widows?"

Corey nodded. "What did they do to the baker? Steal pies, at the very least. At the blacksmith? Frighten the horses and try to make them trample the poor farrier? At the inn? Sneak in the kitchen and dump pepper in the stew? Hard to imagine the limits they would not dare to breach."

Elaine was beginning to show the hint of a smile. "While the shopgirls were busy helping their mamas, I imagine they pulled the ribbons off their spools and tangled them all up."

Corey could not help a little grin. "I am ashamed to

allow myself to find amusement in our exaggerations. I hope they have exhausted their list of youthful follies and we will be spared more foolish stories."

Despite her words, Corey suspected many more dinners like the one they had just survived were in store.

Four

Matt watched the two ladies walk from the room, their dignity intact. The conversation could not have been agreeable for them, but not even Perry seemed to notice.

When the men settled in the library for port and smoking, Alfred chose a cigar from the box held by Oakley. "Fine-looking chit, that Miss B-Bransford. You still interested, Cedric?" Alfred rolled the cigar carefully in his fingers, sniffing deeply before holding it to a flame.

Matt leaned forward to catch the reply, but Cedric only shrugged.

Perry's lips curved in a sly smile. "She refused you once, did she not? I seem to recall that when I decided to marry Elaine, you thought about jumping into the parson's mousetrap yourself, right, Cedric?"

Matt well remembered Cedric's attraction to Miss Bransford. If Cedric had not first expressed his interest in her those five years ago, Matt might have courted the young lady himself. But would he have proposed marriage? No, hardly. Matt had been far more interested in advancing his military career in those days. But Cedric had tried, of that Matt was certain.

"Well, Cedric?" Alfred was puffing away, but not ready

to let the subject die. As always among the Quartet, competition to josh one another was intense.

Cedric's scowl deepened. "Stubble it, all of you. That was eons ago and meant nothing."

"But if she had accepted, you would have had a wife to support, is that not so?" asked Alfred.

"All right, Alfred, you nodcock, you are technically correct. But I knew she would never leave her parents. They depended on her, and still do, unless I miss my guess."

"Then what was she doing in London that year? And what is she doing here?"

"Demmed if I know. Just know she said they needed her. Something about a rascal of a brother always in debt and breaking their hearts with his carousing."

Alfred blew a cloud of smoke. "Just like you, Cedric—is that what you are saying?"

"Her brother was so bad he took off for Canada or New York, someplace he could make a new start."

"Or follow his inclinations to make a fortune by less than honorable means," Perry said.

Alfred studied his ash. "Miss Bransford is a very p-pretty little thing."

"Yes, but a bit too proper and prim for my taste," Cedric said.

"Oh, have you given this some thought?"

"Well, I rather have." Cedric shook his head. "But she no longer appeals to me."

"Ha!" Alfred laughed out loud. "I noticed your looks at her. Do not try to c-convince me you are not interested in her, my friend."

"But not for marriage! I have decided against it altogether. Not my dish of tea, as they say."

"And might I ask what you find so unattractive about

the state of matrimony?" Perry's voice was light, but his eyes seemed hard and a tiny frown drew his brows together.

"Why, nothing at all if I had the blunt. But I am not always quite up to the mark at every bill. I sometimes wonder . . ."

"Perhaps you have cultivated the wrong habits. That was an expensive bit of fluff you were keeping last winter."

Cedric heaved a deep sigh. "You said it true! Far too expensive. I was delighted when Rhodes made his offer to take her off my hands."

Alfred gave a gruff laugh. "You don't have to offer marriage to Miss Bransford. But you might have a bit of f-fun with her."

Matt snapped back to attention. "Fun? I hope you are not talking something dishonorable here, Alfred."

"Not dishonorable, no, of course not. But the gel is on the shelf. Might enjoy a bit of f-flirtation, would you not agree? Harmless sort of thing."

Cedric shook his head. "Or not so harmless, if she traps me into wedding her."

Alfred grinned. "Ah, where is your nerve and your spirit of fun? Your s-sense of adventure?"

Fun? Matt was beginning to find the conversation most distasteful. He changed the subject. "You never did tell us, Perry. Is that big old trout still there, the one we could never catch?"

"There is a monster-size trout in that hole. Whether he is the same one as before, I sincerely doubt. But I have seen him—glimpses only, of course. If one of us managed to hook him, it would be a great victory, one we've sought for many years."

They poured another round of claret and called for

another bottle, laughing now at how the old fish had outfoxed them year after year, showing himself just often enough to tease them, to make them yearn to set a hook in his mouth.

"Twenty guineas one of us lands him this year!" Cedric drew on his cigar.

"Double that!"

Perry pulled out their old betting book from a cabinet behind his desk.

They laughed and exclaimed over the entries, going back to their youth. Most numerous were the wagers on the fish, but many others, even on billiards, filled the pages.

Alfred pointed at page after page. "Matt outpaced all of us. He had the largest catch almost every year."

Cedric chortled at the archery results. "Unless you have been practicing daily, Perry, you will again occupy the bottom of the list."

Perry arched his eyebrows. "And do I not recall you never won a footrace, Cedric?"

A chorus of laughter greeted each line. Finally, Perry turned to a blank page, dipped his quill, and wrote the date at the top. He held his hand poised over the empty page.

"Ten guineas I land the first trout." Matt started the ball rolling.

The third bottle of claret disappeared and the fourth was decanted before the rapid delivery of bets slowed.

"And tell me, Cedric, how much would you like to wager that you b-breach Miss Bransford's fortifications in the next f-four weeks?"

Matt drew in a quick breath. This was atrocious! But Cedric and Perry guffawed.

Cedric sputtered as he spoke. "Without getting leg-shackled, that is."

Perry held up a hand. "Wait, you must define your terms. What does 'breaching her fortifications' mean, Alfred, you lecherous old toad?"

Matt rose. "You cannot mean taking her virtue, Alfred. That would be outside of enough."

Alfred gave a derisive snort. "Don't be a spoilsport, Matt. She is old enough to take c-care of herself. And should have had enough experience. I say if you can kiss her more than five times, that would win my money."

Cedric grinned. "Five times? On separate occasions?"

"And who will verify that accomplishment, I ask you?" Perry asked.

Alfred repeated his sniff. "Well, the rest of us ain't g-going to be there."

Matt sank back into his chair. It really should not be his concern. As they said, Cordelia Bransford ought to be able to take care of herself. And if Cedric's seduction were limited to mere kisses, it would be harmless.

Unless, of course, she lost her heart to Cedric, a condition from which she had not suffered in her London Season, if he recalled accurately. He had danced with her many times, found her quite appealing. But Cedric had declared his intentions first.

Just the same, he felt a little sorry for her now, the unsuspecting butt of their little wagers. Foolish of him. Seemed typical of the crybaby he had become since his brief experience at Waterloo. That the battle had changed his outlook on life was almost a given, though he was still fighting the effects of his new sensibilities. How he hated his little missish tendencies, his pity so quickly engaged over the smallest slight. Like this afternoon, when all he had thought about was that the goose girl was not harmed. Instead of laughing off the plight of others, he somehow wanted to help now.

For the time being, besides intending to win a number of the wagers they had made this evening, he planned to watch out for Miss Cordelia Bransford. Protect her from Cedric. And win that wager. "I'll wager a monkey. Five hundred pounds on Miss Bransford!"

Corey crept quietly down the hall toward the breakfast room. She heard no conversation, no clinking spoon stirring a cup, no knife or fork striking china. She breathed a little sigh of relief, went in, and sat down alone.

Elaine was sleeping. So, she assumed, were the members of the Quartet, no doubt recovering from their reunion celebration. Bess had charge of the children's morning meal and activities. For the moment, Corey could sit in the sunny room and enjoy coffee and toast without interruption.

Rogers, the underbutler, accepted her simple order and brought a silver pot, filling a delicate cup decorated with pink roses for her.

The pot acted as a distorted mirror, and as Corey gazed at her crooked and elongated reflection, she could not help thinking of how very distorted this visit was turning out to be. She wished she did not have to repeat last night's ordeal. But it appeared most evenings would be spent in the company of the four men. However abominable both she and Elaine viewed the situation, there would be no escape. During the day Corey was certain she could stay out of their way.

She sipped her coffee and gazed out of the window at the green park, serene in the morning brightness. She had another line of defense, another little trick to distance herself from the attention of the men. She opened her cloth bag and took out the carefully folded white fabric which she'd brought along with the idea of making a little dress for Elaine's daughter. Now that another baby was on the way, she could instead make a gown and cap for the new arrival. Sitting with a lap full of cloth and a needle in her hand might discourage overly familiar conversation in the drawing room.

Perhaps she could embellish the pieces with embroidery. She opened her needle case to check her supply.

"Good day, Cordelia."

Cedric's voice caught her by surprise. She stuck her pricked finger into her mouth.

"Sorry. Didn't mean to startle you."

She inspected her finger. "No serious damage."

Cedric pulled out a chair and sat down. "You are up early this morning."

"I am often an early riser." Corey put her sewing supplies back in their bag.

Rogers hurried in with a tray holding a cup for Cedric and a plate of toast.

Cedric wrinkled his nose at the toast. "I will have ham and eggs."

"Yes, sir." The underbutler went back to the kitchen.

Cedric filled his cup, drained it, and poured more before he spoke. "I want to tell you again, Cordelia, how very pleased I am to see you."

"I am sure I cannot imagine . . ." Corey stopped herself delivering a stern set-down. She did not want to say anything to encourage his attentions, nor did she wish to engage his hostility. "That is very kind of you, Mr. Williamson."

"I made a terrible error in not following through and insisting you marry me. You must be the only lady who has ever taken my heart, Miss Bransford."

"Mr. Williamson, your tongue is as facile as ever, but you will pardon me, please, if I doubt the sincerity of your words?"

"You mean they do not ring true, my dear? I assure you, Miss Bransford, I am entirely earnest."

Corey thought his expression entirely disingenuous, despite his smooth words. She drew a deep, slow breath. One ploy always diverted his attention. Let him talk about himself. "Tell me what you have been doing for the last few years, if you please."

Cedric smiled and leaned back in his chair. "My father thought I had the makings of a good diplomat. I went to Russia for a year with the British delegation, but I did not care for the work . . ."

As Cedric spoke, Corey smiled to herself. She could just imagine his father, Lord Clarke, hoping against hope that his youngest son had some skills besides attending *ton* parties and carousing in gaming clubs.

". . . profoundly dull in all regards."

The footman placed a full plate before him, and Cedric paused in his account to take a few bites.

"Listening to endless conversations and struggling to understand that infernal language they spoke. Never had a knack for foreign tongues . . ."

Corey waited while he ate more.

"Glad I got out before that Vienna business. Disappointed the pater, but then . . ."

More ham and eggs.

"If you had not refused me, Cordelia, perhaps I would have been a success in diplomacy."

"Whatever would I have done to improve things?" Corey watched him take another heaping forkful. Just another few minutes, she promised herself, and she could beg his pardon and get away.

Matt let himself into the house by the garden door and headed for breakfast. He hoped his morning walks would quickly build his endurance. Those bets of last night meant he would have to stand up to at least two boxing bouts. He slowed his steps when he heard Cedric speaking from inside the breakfast room.

"A brilliant wife, beautiful and accomplished, would have been a great asset to my career."

Matt halted, listening.

The second voice was Miss Bransford's. "Mr. Williamson, please do not exaggerate. Remember, you never made me a formal offer, so I never refused you. Nor am I beautiful or accomplished. If you are trying to make me feel guilty, you will have a very hard time of it."

Matt frowned as he heard the scrunch of a chair being moved.

Cedric's voice was lower now. "Have you no feelings for me? You know I was never suited for the military or the Church."

"So what are you doing these days? Oh, yes, Rogers, just a little more coffee, please."

Matt was relieved they were not alone.

Cedric spoke again. "I am going to take over one of my father's minor properties. He thinks I can manage. My prospects, he says, are quite bright, as I am a particular favorite of my Aunt Amelia. She is likely to leave me a handsome fortune."

"How very fortunate you are, Mr. Williamson."

"You used to call me Cedric."

"That was a long time ago."

"You used to like my kisses, Corey."

"What kisses?"

"I remember, even if you do not."

"What tarradiddle. Now, move away, Mr. Williamson."

Matt had heard far too much already. He gave a loud cough and strode into the breakfast room.

Miss Bransford leaned away from Cedric, who had moved his chair next to hers and was about to cover her hand in kisses. As soon as Matt entered, Cedric dropped her hand and picked up his cup.

"Mornin', Matt."

Miss Bransford gave him a cool glance that Matt chose to interpret as grateful.

"Good day, Cedric. Miss Bransford." Matt lifted the cup Rogers poured for him and took a sip. "I hope, Miss Bransford, you were not appalled at our conversation last evening."

She looked him straight in the eye and paused for a moment before she spoke. "I suppose you pulled down the laundry maid's clean sheets and dragged them through the dirt, too."

Matt grinned, though he felt the sting of her words. "How did we ever miss such an opportunity for a prank, Cedric?"

Miss Bransford was not finished. "You did not tell any stories of bringing elderly ladies cups of lemonade with fish swimming in them. Or seed cakes made with baked insects."

"No. Apparently our repertoire was limited. We

could have profited by having a clever girl like you with us," Matt said.

Cedric guffawed. "Cordelia, you are a sly puss. Indeed you are."

"And now, if you gentlemen will excuse me, I have a rendezvous with Lord Henry and Lady Georgina."

When she was gone, Matt dug into his plate of eggs. In between bites he caught Cedric's eye. "My friend, I think Miss Bransford just delivered us a particularly sharp set-down."

"Yes, but I am not discouraged."

Matt wondered if Cedric truly had confidence in his appeal or if he spoke mostly bluster. "You like a female with spirit?"

He didn't care much for the tone of Cedric's derisive laugh.

Matt shoved the last of the eggs into his mouth. Other than Rogers's presence serving the breakfast, Cedric had been alone with Corey, not a situation Matt should allow to happen if he could prevent it. "I think I will head out to see how Zeus has adapted to his new surroundings. We are going down to the river later to check progress of the mayflies, right?"

"So Perry said." With nonchalance, Cedric picked up yesterday's newspaper and turned to the racing report.

Matt walked to the stables, taking care not to favor the weaker leg, but instead of going to his horse's stall, he looked around to see if anyone was paying attention to him before he ducked into the carriage house. All was silence and near darkness as he went to the largest barouche and climbed in. He eased off his boot, stretched out on the soft upholstery, and propped his sore leg up on the open window. Kept the swelling down, some apothecary had told him, if he elevated it for an hour or two every day. At home, where his mother and sisters had plagued him with their inflated ministrations, he had discovered a refuge in the quiet of the empty carriage house. He'd never been discovered. No reason he would be found here, either.

He raised his arms, placed them behind his head, and let a wry smile curve his lips. Miss Bransford had been very quiet last evening. But this morning, she showed just what she thought of their reminiscences. He couldn't blame her. Four grown men reliving youthful mischief, bragging about how foxed they had been on this night or that. Lady Elaine's expression had shown her displeasure, but Miss Bransford had borne it all with stoic aplomb. Or so it had appeared until a half-hour ago. Her pointed remarks had put him and Cedric in their places, right next to the clowns, buffoons, and jesters. Her tone was as stern as an elderly governess confronting her wayward charge. Perhaps too stern.

Matt shifted his leg to the left a bit. Held up like this, the old wound throbbed less. Damn lucky he had been conscious enough to prevent the surgeon from sawing off the whole leg. And damn lucky his body fought off the infection, though it had eaten away a large section of his thigh muscle. Just damn lucky.

His mind drifted back to Miss Bransford. Was she lucky? Lucky to have escaped the whim of Cedric to wed her five years ago? Or unlucky to remain a spinster instead of finding an eligible match? She was pretty enough, though she apparently had a sharp tongue and a willingness to use it.

Even so, Matt detested the way Cedric treated her.

Leering at her, almost sitting on top of her, making suggestive remarks about old kisses.

Kisses!

Had he not teased Miss Bransford in precisely the same way last night? His stomach felt uneasy and his neck felt hot as a flush spread to his face. How could he have been such a rattlepate?

He was no better than Cedric. Or any other rake-hellish old lecher. He felt the flush of shame burn his cheeks.

Of course, he had thought his remarks meaningless flirtation. Probably what Cedric thought, too. Devil take it, things looked different when one gave them more than trifling thought. This morning, Cedric had leaned over Miss Bransford, practically drooling in his eagerness, eyes bright as though he disrobed her in his head. No wonder the lady held Cedric in a minimum of regard.

Matt knew she felt the same way about him, too. Clever girl!

Cedric would have a tough time bringing her to heel, or he missed his guess. Nevertheless, Matt would keep a watchful eye on her. Cedric would probably tickle the bounds of propriety. Though he did not have a mean bone in his body, old Ceddy easily got carried away when he fought to win a wager.

Matt would be the soul of decorum from now on. That, he promised himself!

Corey stopped by Elaine's boudoir on her way from breakfast to the nursery. "Good morning, Elly. How did you sleep?"

Elaine frowned at the plate of toast on her tray. "I felt

all right last night, but the bilious attack is back this morning. I cannot abide the sight of food, not even this crust of toast. Can you please set it on the chair, Corey?"

"Of course."

"Perhaps I overdid that dinner. Perry has offered to take the men to the Red Lion in the village tonight. We can have a light supper together and enjoy ourselves alone."

Corey felt a combination of welcome delight and a touch of inexplicable disappointment. She quickly concealed the pang of regret. Wherever had it come from? "The plan sounds wonderful. Just think—no more stories about childish pranks." But neither would there be the very handsome Lord Matthew in his black evening coat.

Corey shook off her ambivalence. "We will have a wonderful coze, cousin. I can tell you about my adventures with Henry and Gina."

"Are you taking them on another jaunt? I am so sorry they are so ill-behaved. When Nurse left, they became sulky and naughty."

"As I told you, I have no expectations for them at all. Everything they do is a surprise to me."

"I know I will be a better mother when I get over these bouts of queasiness."

"Of course you will, Elly."

"Do not overexert yourself, darling Corey. And make Bess pay attention to the children. I suspect she is thinking about some village boy when she should be concentrating on Henry and Gina."

Corey gave Elaine a little kiss on the cheek and went upstairs to the nursery.

The children were not yet fully dressed, and as they had yesterday, they poked and teased one another while Bess seemed helpless to stop them. Articles of clothing were strewn about the room.

Corey drew a deep breath. "Children, please pick up all the clothes on the floor and give them to Bess. I will be ready to go out when you are dressed. If you cannot cooperate with Bess, then we will not go." She turned away from them and shut her ears to their arguments.

She went to the window and looked out at the gardens below. Something Cedric had said came back into her head. How had he put it? He thought he would inherit money from his aunt? Was that not just like Cedric, to fall into more good luck? He might even become wealthy, though he had not named an amount of the potential legacy.

Then again, if he was able, he would probably gamble it all away or spend it on horses and loose women.

This summer was turning out to be miserable. The children. The Quartet and their competitions. Cedric and his unwelcome attentions.

But if Cedric inherited, and if she encouraged his attentions, and if she became his wife, would there be enough money to keep her parents in Bath?

No, a thousand times no. She would rather be a companion to some cranky old lady than put up with Cedric! Even a governess to a couple of children as irritating as Henry and Gina would be better.

Though if she lived in the country on that estate Cedric's father gave him . . . and if she had her own children to enjoy . . . would that be so terrible? A family of her own, even if the father was usually in town, off chasing foxes or who knew what else?

Gina gave a sharp cry and Corey turned around to see Bess trying to brush the child's hair. Henry sat on the floor fumbling with the buckles on his shoes. "Bess, if you help Henry with his shoes, I will see if I can brush Gina's hair."

"No, no." Gina's cry was relatively soft.

Corey took the brush from Bess and knelt beside Gina, taking her arm as she started to crawl away. "Here, dear, we want to make your hair pretty. Look at these lovely curls."

Gina turned her big blue eyes on Corey with surprise. "Pretty?"

Corey gently brushed the ends of Gina's hair, carefully separating the tangles with her fingers. "Tonight we can braid your hair, just as your mama does, to prevent these snarls."

Gina did not look pleased, but at least she stopped crying and wiped away her tears with a chubby hand. Corey could sort out the remaining tangles later.

Henry accepted Bess's help with his shoe buckles, and in moments they were ready.

"Now we will visit Baby Lawrence. Then, if you two are very, very good, we shall have a picnic luncheon." Both children looked suspicious, but willing to test her.

Later, Corey congratulated herself on a successful outing. The children had behaved well at Mrs. Hitchens's cottage, taking Corey to see the puppies and even cooing over their little brother. When they had arrived at the duck pond on the home farm, they found a wagonload of food and a table and chairs set up in the partial shade of a newly leafed beech. Corey had ordered a simple meal and a rug to spread on the ground. Instead of the little picnic she anticipated, two footmen stood at attention next to the table, ready to set out the food.

Nevertheless, Corey insisted on sitting on the rug with the children and leaving the table empty. The novelty seemed to fascinate Gina and Henry. Both ate without complaining, surprising even Bess, who must have been quite accustomed to their resistance.

When they were finished, Corey sent Henry on a walk to the far side of the pond and back with one of the footmen while the other packed up the remnants of the food. Gina curled up in Bess's lap and fell asleep.

In this moment of tranquility, Corey leaned against the tree trunk and gazed over the scene. To the right were ancient stone buildings, still serving the purposes for which they were built several hundred years ago. Reeds at the water's edge were still low and a soft green, marking the transition from the long meadow grass to the soft blue of the pond. A few bright yellow cowslips still bloomed not far from the first of the bluebells. In the distance, the fields were dotted with white blossoms. On the water, the ducklings paddled in straight lines after their mamas.

Corey's thoughts floated back to Cedric and his prospects. Despite the chance he would come into more luck than he deserved, he would make a terrible husband, undependable and often absent, following his caprices, flitting from one thing to another, handsome and charming but irresponsible. Worse was his propensity for gambling.

Cedric was suited for nothing but endless trouble. Rather than having a calling, he had confusion. Rather than a profession, he performed pranks. No, even if he were rich as Croesus, she would be miserable in a loveless marriage. That she even dared to entertain the remote notion of wedding Cedric qualified her for admission to Bedlam.

Five

Matt slowed Zeus from a full gallop to a dancing walk. The horse wanted to run more, but Matt's weak leg troubled him. Not only was it painful, but he wondered what would happen if his foot slipped from the stirrup. Zeus tossed his handsome, dark head as if to ask what had troubled his master for almost a year, a year in which the horse had minimal chances to indulge its instinct to run like the wind.

Matt massaged his thigh and spoke silently to the horse. *Just wait, old boy, we'll have our chances. But for now, I think any race we enter has to be a sprint over a very short distance.* Matt tried to fight off the pain, box it up and forget it, but even though he could try to rise above the aches, the leg was weak. Too weak for a cross-country race next week. He would have to take a route different from the others and pretend Zeus threw a shoe.

They headed into a copse of birch trees, avoiding the main park surrounding the house, and Zeus lapsed into a flat-footed walk. *Poor fellow, you gave up on me.*

Matt let his mind wander back to the breakfast room. Could she have sought Cedric's company? Had Cedric come in after Miss Bransford was already there? Or had she joined him at the table? From her reaction, such a situation seemed quite unlikely. But perhaps Miss Bransford, deep down, regretted she had not married. Perhaps she wanted to encourage Cedric to come up to scratch. Was that possible? How could he find out, other than asking her outright?

When they broke out of the trees, Matt saw the home farm buildings in the distance and a little closer, a cluster of people near a pond. As he approached them, he saw it was Miss Bransford with two children, sitting on a rug under a huge tree. They were accompanied by several servants, a wagon with its horses, and a pony attached to the strangest cart he had ever seen.

As Matt rode up to them, the little boy, apparently Perry's heir, waved at him. Miss Bransford looked around and followed suit.

Miss Bransford had removed her bonnet and the sunshine fell on her hair, turning it a lovely shade of gold. She gave him a broad smile. "Good day, Lord Matthew. Would you care to join us for a little luncheon?"

Lord Henry jumped to his feet and approached Zeus. "Is this your best horse, the battle charger?"

Matt nodded at the boy, then spoke to Miss Bransford. "A cool drink would certainly be in order."

The groom took the horse's reins as Matt carefully swung to the ground. "He might take a bit of water, if you please, and a bit of walking."

Matt did not allow himself to favor his bad leg as he took a chair rather than trying to sit on the ground.

Miss Bransford smiled up at him. "I asked Cook to prepare a little picnic for us, and look what they sent—a whole load of tables and chairs and enough food for a dozen or more."

Bess set several dishes beside him on the table and

Miss Bransford joined him, sitting in a chair on the opposite side.

She folded her hands before her. "I particularly recommend one of those tarts. I see Henry admires your horse, Lord Matthew."

Matt squinted at the groom holding the reins as Zeus drank from the pond. "Is the boy horse-mad? Many little boys adore the beasts."

"He talks about getting a pony for his birthday, but how could any boy resist such a magnificent specimen as your mount?"

"He is a fine animal. Irish-bred, they said when I bought him."

"Is he a recent purchase, then?"

"Oh no, he was with me in . . . for many years." He hated to mention the words 'Belgium' or 'Waterloo', for everyone immediately wanted to hear of his exploits. Matt had not the slightest desire to talk of the battle or its aftermath. The images were still too raw, too ugly. He picked up a tart and bit into it. The sweet juice instantly made him forget anything but its delicious taste.

"Were you horse-mad as a boy, Lord Matthew?"

He swallowed. "I was. Do you ride, Miss Bransford?"

"Not for the last few years. We used to have . . ." She let her voice fade away.

As he devoured the rest of the tart, he thought she looked sad for a moment, but before he could comment, she turned to the little girl, who sat up, rubbing her eyes.

Miss Bransford motioned the child to her side and took her hand. "This is Lord Matthew, Lady Georgina. Make your curtsy, my dear."

Bashfully, the child spread her skirt and dipped a little bow to him. She was adorable.

"I am most honored to make your acquaintance, Lady Georgina. And I assume that rascal petting my horse is your brother."

Gina's blond curls tumbled over her forehead as she tucked in her chin and nodded shyly. Matt could see she would be a beauty in another fifteen years or so.

Miss Bransford called to Henry and he scampered back to the picnic to be formally introduced.

Matt stood and returned the boy's sober bow. "I am pleased to know you, Lord Henry. Do you like Zeus?"

"Almost as much as Flyer, my father's best stallion."

Matt grinned. "Well, that is understandable. Now, would you like to assist that groom in walking Zeus until he is cooled off?"

"Could I?"

Miss Bransford touched Henry's shoulder. "May I?"

"May I?"

Matt agreed and waved him away. "Do you enjoy being with the children, Miss Bransford? You seem to have a knack for it."

"Frankly, I know nothing about children, Lord Matthew. So far I have succeeded in helping Elaine only by using bribes to make them behave. I believe my techniques could use considerable refinement."

Her candor surprised him. Did not all ladies know about taking care of infants? "I have little experience with children myself."

She ruffled Georgina's pale gold hair. "I am trying to help Elaine. The children's nurse was called away unexpectedly."

Again, Matt was reminded of his uncertainty about

her interest in Cedric. If she wanted marriage and children of her own, he was a handsome catch, from a good family, though careless with his blunt. He had to work around to the topic with care. "Have you visited Elaine frequently here at Lodesham?"

"I am afraid not. This is my first trip south from Yorkshire since I was in London five years ago."

So she had led a quiet life? Of course, she might have been courted by a local man. "If you will excuse my impertinent curiosity, Miss Bransford, I will tell you I am surprised you have not married."

Unless his eyes deceived him, a faint blush appeared on her cheeks.

He pressed on. "I thought Cedric would come up to scratch back then. But he claims you discouraged him."

"Indeed I did. Mr. Williamson might make some lady a fine husband, but he and I would not suit."

"Are you certain? Please excuse my prying. You have no need to answer if the subject offends you."

Her voice had a stony quality that told Matt he was treading close to the edge. "I am not offended by your question, Lord Matthew. But I would ask you in return, do you think Mr. Williamson would be a good husband? I see him as a scapegrace, a jokester, a gambler. I cannot see that we would have any interests in common."

"I am sorry to have broached the subject. I, of course, am quite fond of Cedric, one of my oldest friends. I suppose I understand your reservations, but it is usually assumed that a man settles down a bit when he marries, is that not so?"

She lightly touched his arm. "I do not mean to malign your friend. I am sure he is an admirable companion for you."

He wanted to draw her hand back, to press it close. "Oh, no offense, Miss Bransford. None at all, and I would be most appreciative if you take no umbrage at my improper queries."

She nodded, her face brightening in a smile. The breeze blew a few golden strands of hair across her face. She swept them behind her ear, but they instantly fluttered back. He almost had to grab one hand with the other to keep from reaching to her face to brush them away again. He got to his feet. "Well, I think I should collect Henry and show him how to catch a frog. I think that is how most bantlings start our lives of mischief, chasing our sisters or our governesses with amphibians. Or do you wish to prevent Henry from following in our footsteps?"

She grinned. "When you put it that way, Lord Matthew, my disapproval sounds petty. Even futile."

He reached for her wayward hair, but caught himself in time, turning it into a shrug. "All boys, even the members of the Quorn Quartet, eventually outgrow their pranks. Though we may feel remorse when we remember how carefree our youth was." He gave her a little smile, then called to Henry. "I say, Henry, I think Zeus is cooled down. Are there any frogs around this pond?"

Corey glared at the sprigged muslin gown she spread across the bed. Elaine had said not to dress for dinner, but this old thing seemed more like a dress she would wear to put up preserves or concoct an infusion of herbs than to dine with her dear cousin, who always wore perfect ensembles from London's most exclusive modistes.

Corey hung the gown in the clothes press and stared at the meager choices before her. With a scowl, she grabbed a light blue silk, new fully three years ago. It would have to do.

She heard the hooves of several horses crunching outside on the driveway and discreetly peeked out to see the grooms leading four mounts to the door. Perry, Cedric, Lord Matthew, and Mr. Collingwood came down the steps from the house. She moved quickly back into the shadows. She did not wish them to look up and see her. In a few moments, they moved away on horseback, off to the inn. As always, they appeared full of good humor, in high spirits.

She watched them disappear around a curve. Why had Lord Matthew asked her about Cedric that afternoon? She hoped her lack of interest had been clear. The last thing she wanted was for anyone to think she came to Lodesham Hall to capture Cedric.

Other than his probing questions, Lord Matthew had been all that was polite. Had she inadvertently revealed her attraction to him? She ran over their conversation in her head. Nothing she remembered would have given away her secret fascination. From now on, she must be doubly, triply cautious when he was around. This visit was difficult enough without someone like Elaine trying to interest Lord Matthew in a nobody like her.

Dinner with Elaine would simply be a nice coze between two old friends. They need not mention Lord Matthew or Cedric at all. Elaine had no inkling how she felt. Corey squared her shoulders, drew a deep breath, and went downstairs.

Elaine waited for Corey at a small table in the green saloon, a little room decorated in shades of gray-green with ivory and gilt walls. "This is my favorite place to sit and read, Corey. So I had Oakley set it for dinner."

"Elaine, it is lovely. Have you chosen everything here?"

"Yes. It is the only room on this floor in which I changed the old décor. I brought the things I love most in here."

On a side table sat an orchestra of porcelain monkeys, dressed in the fashion of the last century. One of them held a baton while the others held a violin, a cello, a flute, and other instruments.

Corey leaned down for a closer look.

Elaine drew a finger over the drummer. "Are they not quaint? Perry's grandmama had exquisite taste. Almost everything in this house was chosen by her. She worked closely with Mr. Adam, the architect. Not even Perry's mother dared to change the designs they created."

"I can see why you love these little monkeys. How are you feeling?"

"Fine, this evening. Though I must retire early. By morning I expect to feel quite vile all over again."

"Is it any comfort to know the nausea will go away?"

"Not much. The hours crawl by in the morning. But enough of that. Please tell me about your picnic. Where did you go?"

"First I took the children to see Lawrence again. Elly, he is a darling baby, happy and gurgling."

"Mrs. Hitchens nursed Henry, too. She is very good with the babies."

"I like her. Her cottage smells delicious. Yesterday she had just baked bread. Today she had two fruit pies cooling on the windowsill. And she gave us tarts for our picnic."

"You mean Cook did not send along enough food?"

"Oh, more than enough. Too much, in fact. Plus a table and chairs and footmen to serve us. But Mrs. Hitchens's tarts were still warm." Corey remembered the sweet berries and how they slid down her throat. And how could she forget the look of bliss on Lord Matthew's face when he tasted them?

"Have a glass of sherry. We do not have to be on our best behavior this evening without anyone to see us. We can giggle just as we used to do."

Corey took the glass of sherry from the side table and sipped it. Compared to the fruit tart, this was second class, even though she knew Perry described it as the best Spain produced.

"I have been thinking about you, Corey. Is it not time for you to consider marriage?"

"Pooh. I have yet to meet a gentleman who tempts me to leave the single state." Corey was only half fibbing. How could one count a full-fledged aristocrat like Lord Matthew as a potential suitor for a village vicar's daughter, whatever her distant connections?

"But you cannot stay with your parents indefinitely. Is there no eligible *parti* near you in Yorkshire? Certainly you must attend local assemblies from time to time."

"Believe me when I say I have met no one of interest, Elly. My mother saw to it that I was thrust in the way of any potential husbands, not that there were many. Men like females who simper and hide behind their fans. I am too ordinary."

"You cannot mean it. You are lovely, accomplished, and clever. You will make a perfect wife for . . ." Elaine paused.

"For the right gentleman," Corey finished Elaine's

sentence and shook her head slowly. "Where is the right gentleman?"

"Perhaps your standards are unreasonable. You may expect too much of marriage. Love is only part of the equation."

"I understand that love can grow with time and nurturing." Five years without any contact with Lord Matthew had probably heightened her feeling for him. What would close proximity have done?

"Then what is wrong with Cedric? He is handsome and charming."

"You are the third person to push me toward Cedric this very day, Elaine. First, the man himself—then Lord Matthew, now you. As I told the others, we would never suit. He is irresponsible and silly. I cannot respect him, certainly the first requirement for a successful match."

"But men change, you know. Once they have wives, they view the world differently."

"I think his mama should have disciplined him twenty years ago. Then it might have done some good."

Elaine shrugged. "I admit I have said some awful things about him, but no worse than the others. As a group, they are dreadful. As individuals, they are rather appealing."

"Elly, I cannot believe my ears. You, who shed tears at their arrival? Now you think I should marry Cedric Williamson?"

"Let us be seated at the table, Corey." She rang a little silver bell. "When we have been served, we can talk about it again."

Corey took her chair and watched in silence as Oakley and Rogers placed several dishes among the candles and silver on the table. Elaine kept up a cheery commentary on the food and the talents of her chef.

When they were alone, Elaine returned to the subject Corey dreaded. "Just think about marriage, Corey. Otherwise, what will you do? Go to Bath with your mother and father? What could life be like there for a single lady of your youth? Good heavens, the dowager goes to Bath. That is enough to prove the place unlivable!"

Corey gave a bitter laugh. She could imagine herself at dinner in Bath with the dowager—any dowager, as a matter of fact. Such a dinner could hardly be more unpleasant than this one with her cousin, could it?

Elaine continued. "Do you have a bit of money of your own?"

"No. As I told you, Father sends every spare cent to Georgie."

"Then I think you have no choice, Corey. You must marry."

"Elly, you could not possibly wish me such grief as to push me into wedding a man like Cedric. I would rather be a companion to some old lady!"

Elaine's fork clattered onto her plate. "No! You cannot be considering such a thing. I cannot imagine . . ." Her voice faded as she stared at Corey with incredulity.

"I . . . I do not see any other way."

"Has your father no savings?"

Corey shook her head. "Not a groat. Georgie is trying to make a new start, but his schemes seem to lead nowhere."

"Oh, Corey, I had no idea. No wonder you have not been back to London. But even if your parents send all their extra money to your brother, the three of you have to live. Surely there is some source of money. You cannot think of taking employment!"

Why had Corey let that little slip into the conversation? She never meant for Elaine or anyone else to know of her plans. Not even her mother and father were to be included in her strategy. She did not know quite how, but she intended to arrange their living accommodations in Bath without their knowledge of the source of the funds. Now Corey wanted nothing more than to suppress Elaine's concern.

"Father will have a small pension, but he must give up the vicarage when the new man comes in October. Perhaps something will come along to help out."

Elaine bristled. "Something? Cordelia, I suspect that *something* will be you. That is your intention, is it not?"

"I wish we could talk about anything but the future, Elaine. Gina looks so very much like you."

"Bother Gina. This is serious. Do you intend to hire yourself out as a companion and send every penny to keep your parents in Bath while they are sending everything they have to Georgie? What utter madness!"

"Elly, please do not exaggerate. It was just a thought I had. A way to help Father and Mother."

Elaine sank back in her chair with a skeptical look. "I certainly hope it was just a whim and you never think about it again. The idea!"

Too late, Corey realized the implications of what she had blurted out. She never meant to say a word about her idea to seek a position. But now she had spilled the plan without thinking. "I will probably not—"

"I certainly hope not. Your parents would be appalled at such a thing."

Corey needed to change the topic of conversation. If Elaine truly believed Corey would hire herself out, she and Perry would be aghast. The next thing Corey knew, she would be offered a competence to stay here and care for the children. Corey refused to allow herself to become an object of pity.

But Elaine was not finished. "Corey, what is wrong with marrying Cedric?"

She could not help giving a direct answer. "Other than the fact he is not interested in marrying me? He has no money except an allowance from his father, most of which is gambled away before the next quarter. Cedric is sometimes charming, too handsome for his own good, and entirely untrustworthy. Why would I tie my future to such a fellow?"

"When you say that, I must agree. But what of Lord Matthew or Alfred? You said something a while ago about Lord Matthew asking you about Cedric. Why was he asking?"

"Oh, it was nothing. I really do not recall—"

"Corey, I have watched Matthew when he looks at you. I think, if you gave him the slightest encouragement . . ."

"Please, Elly, let us talk of anything else. When I hear about the capers those fellows so revere, I think I never want to be near a man again!" She hoped the fluttery feeling she felt when Elly spoke of Matthew was not evident to anyone but Corey herself.

Elaine's hand flew to her throat. "Cordelia! Now what are you saying?"

"Oh, I do not know. I wish I could go to France and enter a convent." Corey felt the tears gathering and a lump grow in her throat.

Elaine set down her silver and took Corey's hand in hers. "I think I am beginning to understand, cousin dear. You think all men are like Georgie, worthless and completely irresponsible. No wonder you do not wish to marry."

Corey fought back her urge to collapse in Elaine's arms and sob out her heart. Elaine had the truth of it. "I do not despise all men. There are many who take their duties seriously. Why, oh why, could George not be like our father?" She dabbed at the tears and twisted her handkerchief.

"No one can answer for George, Corey. I should think he would be ashamed to need money from his family. What is he trying to do in Canada?"

"He writes of various investments he has made, none of which is successful. From his letters, his life sounds all that is proper. But I suspect he is not telling the truth. I fear he indulges his propensity for moving with the monied crowd, gambling and drinking. Just like he did in London, wasting his money and never learning to make his own way in the world."

"Your parents should cut him off, not send another penny."

"And so I have told them, which sends my mother into spasms and sends Father off to brood in solitude."

"And puts you quite out of favor."

Corey summoned a half smile. "Yes. Entirely so."

Elaine sighed and rang a little silver bell. "We shall have our sweetmeats now. For the rest of the evening we shall talk of nothing but pleasantries, dearest. And later, we can play together. I have not played my harp for weeks now, but I am sure I have not forgotten."

Corey nodded. She prayed Elaine *would* forget her inadvertent revelation about finding employment. Corey was determined to seek her own solution to helping her parents without interference, however well-intentioned.

* * *

Corey wrapped her shawl around her shoulders and sat on the stone bench in the rose garden. She had awakened early after a night of uneasy sleep. Instead of an evening of shared confidences, the dinner with Elaine turned out to be a difficult experience. Even when she had played the harpsichord and Elaine her harp, the music sounded unharmonious, uneven, from time to time dissonant.

Corey had ascertained that the rose garden was not visible from the windows of the bedchambers in which the three men were housed. Not that any of them would arise early. She could safely sit here without fear of being interrupted. Dewdrops sparkled on the leaves and petals as brightly as Elly's diamonds.

A few insects were up early, fluttering from bud to bud. Soon the garden would be ablaze with blooms. How her mother would enjoy seeing Elly's lovely garden. Mama could grow roses in a garden in Bath, if only Corey could get her there.

When her parents had to leave the old vicarage, they could not stay in Mitton Moorby. Her mama worried about how her husband would adjust to his retirement. Too hard for him to stand by and watch another man take over his parish. Mother thought she would not be bothered, but how would she adapt to no longer being the center of the parish ladies, the one who presided at the teas along with the squire's wife, who organized the annual summer fete and the harvest celebrations?

No, it would be difficult for Mother. Her parents needed to be away, in a comfortable atmosphere, where they could be with their friends. And it would be easier for Corey herself to move away if they left, too.

Bath was definitely a place her parents would enjoy, with its many opportunities to see old friends and make new ones, people like them, who enjoyed genteel gatherings, music, and books.

A half-finished letter to her parents sat on her dressing table. Last night she had written a carefully edited account of events at Lodesham Hall. No mention of the three male visitors. No mention of Elaine's condition. No mention of the necessity of her caring for the children.

Here in the quiet garden she had the perfect opportunity to put together some lines for the next letter. Mama would expect at least one a sennight. She took a little notebook from her pocket and touched the tip of the pencil to her tongue, prepared to describe the closest bush. A few blooms had opened, fat and ruffled, the pink a deeper shade at the center. The cascade of roses over the old stone wall showed a mix of crimson and white buds.

Not very descriptive words. The glossy dark green of the leaves contrasted with the delicate blush pink of another bush. She supposed the gardener might know the names, and her mother would enjoy hearing them. She put down her pencil.

A pair of bees spiraled around one another, diving and scrambling in their passion to draw the nectar from the blossom's center. They had a firm purpose to their lives and nothing would stand in their way. Unlike Cedric and Matt and Alfred. The bees' competition was an expression of their life force, not a compensation for the vacancy of their heads, the meaningless of their existence.

How was her life any more meaningful than theirs? She was about to do the unthinkable and look for gainful employment. She cringed at the memory of what she had foolishly confessed to Elaine.

How could she erase her confession last night? She cringed at the memory of her accidental remarks about employment. But surely with all Elaine had to worry about, she would not remember.

Yes, she would.

Corey bit her lip, then leaned in to sniff the rosebuds but got more of the odor of the earth, heavy and dark. No exotic scents quite yet.

A faint sound, just like a human sigh, made Corey jump.

"Ahhhh . . ."

Was it a gardener, up early? Or an animal? She stood and walked toward the sound, which came again, a little louder.

"Ahhh . . ."

When she turned the corner of the boxwood hedge, she saw Lord Matthew, sitting on a bench and rubbing one thigh just above his knee.

"You! You are not the gardener!" She blurted the words without thinking.

He got to his feet, standing crookedly. "Miss Bransford. You are quite correct. I am not the gardener."

Six

Miss Bransford was catching him in a bad moment, Matt thought, with his leg feeling especially painful in the morning damp. He was as surprised as she was to meet this early. He could have gone to the carriage house, but instead he had cut through the garden, found this bench, and obviously disturbed Miss Bransford's untimely stroll. "I beg your pardon, Miss Bransford."

"Lord Matthew, what is wrong?"

"Just a cramp in my leg. Nothing much."

She looked skeptical. "You sometimes favor that leg, I believe. Have you injured it?"

Matt paused before he answered. "No, Miss Bransford, it is nothing . . . just . . . nothing."

She moved closer and stood near him. "Did you break it? Or sprain it?"

"No. Please, do not be concerned."

"I believe it pains you, Lord Matthew. Did you fall off your horse?"

He laughed, despite his embarrassment. "Not exactly."

"This is most mystifying. Why are you unwilling to talk about it if you have a strain in your leg?"

"You are a most persistent lady, Miss Bransford."

"I am sorry. I do not mean to pry. Please, you must sit."

He gestured her to go first, then sat beside her. "It is an old war injury. Simply has not quite returned to its original condition."

"And you try to disguise it? Why?"

He shrugged. "If you must know, I don't like to flaunt it. Seems like begging for pity to limp around like someone with a real infirmity."

"I see."

He had the uncomfortable suspicion that she did see, see that he could not bear to admit his weakness.

"I will say nothing. I understand how it is to be . . . well, it will not surprise you to know that I am the poor relation here."

"What are you saying? Poor relation indeed. You are a wonderful friend to Elaine and your help caring for those children is generous of you."

She shook her head. She was so close, the brim of her bonnet bumped his ear.

"Oh, excuse me, I did not mean to . . ."

He reached over, untied the ribbon, lifted off the hat, and set it on the ground. "There. Much better. I like your hair much more than that dangerous straw creation."

She ran her fingers through her long mane in an engaging gesture. He folded his hands around his knee to keep from following hers into those honey-gold tresses.

Corey turned to him with a little smile. "Do you like roses, Lord Matthew?"

"I suppose. I never thought much about them. They are pretty."

"Yes. And fragrant. This garden will be a paradise in a few days when the blooms are fully open."

He laughed. "They must be on the same schedule as the mayflies. We expect the hatch to begin today or tomorrow."

"What is a hatch?"

He explained how all the river creatures were poised to feast when the mayflies unfolded their wings. "The fish and the birds are eager to gobble up the insects. Other predators are waiting to capture the birds and the fish. Which is where we enter the picture. When the trout feed, they are insatiable."

"And you trick them into swallowing your hook instead of the mayfly."

He took her hand and tucked it under his arm, drawing her to her feet. "You understand perfectly, Miss Bransford. And now, may I accompany you to the breakfast room?"

"As you wish, Lord Matthew."

He concentrated on walking evenly, showing not the slightest favor for his bad leg. But he knew it was too late. She already knew the leg bothered him. Matt hoped he could trust her to keep silent.

Corey's heart raced as she walked beside him, her hand warmed by his body, her head full of unintended sensations. Her hat dangled from her other arm and her hair lifted in a puff of wind.

As they walked she wished it were miles to the house, though his leg might not hold up that long. She realized he kept everyone from knowing the extent of his problem because he could not bear to admit he might be less strong and capable since his wounding. She would never humiliate him by exposing the extent of his injury to the other men.

She might even be able to help him. After breakfast, she would check the receipts in the stillroom. There were sure to be the ingredients for a balm she could make to soothe his pain and give him a little relief.

As if he had seen into her thoughts, Lord Matthew gave her hand a little squeeze.

Matt twirled his cue as he watched the downpour outside the billiard room window. The damp made his leg ache worse than usual, with a burning sensation that shot past his knee and down to his toes. He resisted the urge to lean on the stick and ease off his weight.

"Your shot, Matt." Cedric looked gloomily at the water running down the window.

Matt moved deliberately to the table, lining up his next shot. It required a gentle touch, but the ball angled off the cushion a bit too sharply.

Perry watched closely. "Finally you missed one!" He squinted at the table, moving from side to side until he was content. He tapped the ball and it rolled into the pocket.

Alfred blew a cloud of cigar smoke. "Your game, P-Perry. That makes one for me, one for Matt, and one f-for you. Cedric, you are falling b-behind."

Matt edged toward the door, placing his stick in the rack. "You fellows carry on. I will be back shortly."

When no one objected to his departure, Matt went into the corridor and headed for a salon, any place he could sink into a chair and rest the leg. He would have taken refuge in the carriage house, but it was too far on the water-soaked paths. Neither did he feel like climbing the staircase to his bedchamber.

He turned into the Ivory Saloon, where he might find numerous couches on which to stretch out. From an adjacent small chamber came soft laughter.

"And the conductor of the orchestra had to start all over again."

Hearing Miss Bransford's voice, he limped to the doorway and leaned against the wall. Bess sat silently in the corner. Lord Henry and Lady Georgina were wide-eyed as they stared at a set of little figurines on a table. Six china monkeys in powdered wigs were arranged in a semicircle. A conductor in a tailcoat waved a baton, while a pink-gowned singer held a tambourine. Horn, flute, violin, and bass viol players stood near a drummer in a coat of military red with a black tricorn hat. Miss Bransford tapped on the table and spoke in a high tone.

"Attention, monkey orchestra. We will start at the beginning. Is everyone ready?"

Henry turned and met Matt's glance. "Lord Matthew!"

Cordelia looked around and broke into a wide smile.

Matt stepped forward and took a chair near the table. "Do not let me interrupt you."

She pointed her finger at the monkey conductor. "He finally has his players in tune, Lord Matthew. And there the story ends."

Henry grinned. "But the players were ever so naughty. Every one of them broke a bow or lost their music."

Gina chimed in. "The horn player blew away the singer's sheet music."

"My, my," Matt said. "Sometimes it is hard work to manage everyone."

"I know." Gina's pale curls bobbed as she agreed.

"Tell us another story," Henry said.

Miss Bransford ruffled his hair. "Bess is waiting to take you upstairs for your luncheon. I will tell you another story tomorrow."

Henry's face clouded. "But I want to hear one now."

"You must go with Bess. After you eat, you may choose a book and I will read you a story this afternoon. Will that do?"

Henry nodded, though his face wore a petulant pout.

Bess took Gina's hand and led the children out of the room.

Corey leaned back in the chair and cocked her head to one side, contemplating the figurines. "I wonder what the maker of these delicate porcelains would have thought of the silly story I made up."

"He would be delighted to know how people enjoy his handiwork."

"I had a hard time keeping the children from touching them. Elaine would have my head if any of the figurines were broken."

"Elaine is fortunate to have you here willing to spend time with her children."

Corey kept her eyes on the china monkeys, though her smile brought him a grin of his own. "I do not mind. Henry and Gina need someone to let them be children. I fear the nurse, the one who has gone off to care for her mother, is something of a tyrant. They need to be out-of-doors, chasing butterflies and hunting imaginary dragons in the woods."

"I can visualize you chasing butterflies a few years ago, Miss Bransford. Did you also hunt dragons?"

Her eyes twinkled. "Oh, yes. My brother teased me

over and over by telling tales of fire-breathing monsters roving just beyond the first line of trees. I decided to be St. George and, in my imagination, I saved the countryside."

"No wonder I feel such accord with you. I did the very same thing for my village when I was a child. We had a particularly large herd of dragons nearby."

"Were all of yours green? With big, pointy scales all over them?"

"Yes, exactly. I bet we had the same stories read to us. I remember one picture of St. George in which the dragon's many tails were entwined around his mount's legs. I had to defeat those dragons before they could hurt the poor horse."

Their gazes locked for an instant. Her eyes were a soft, sparkling blue, like sunlight on a clear mountain lake. He looked down before he gave in to the urge to take her into his arms.

Corey broke the moment of silence. "I think I remember that exact picture. I will have to see if there is a copy of that volume on the nursery shelves here."

"Please do. I would like to refresh my memory."

She shifted in her chair. "How is your billiard tournament progressing?"

"Sluggishly. We were all set to take on those trout this morning, but this rain put us off."

"Do the fish care? After all, they live underwater."

Matt broke into laughter and she joined in. "Oh, Miss Bransford, that was rare."

When he recovered, he touched her knee. "To tell the truth, the fish do care. Heavy rain riles the river bottom and the water is cloudy, so they cannot see well. And of course the rain retards the mayfly hatch. It is not just our desire to stay dry. If it were a very gentle, misty rain, we would be out there in our oilskins, casting for those trout."

"I am gratified to hear you four are not entirely deterred by the elements."

He gave another bark of laughter.

"Miss Bransford, I find your observations most amusing. I deduce, from your statements, that you find the Quorn Quartet a bit harebrained."

A rosy blush spread over her cheeks and she locked her gaze on the monkey orchestra again. "I respect the bonds of friendship, my lord. Loyalty to one another is a fine thing."

"But those are not all of your views, Miss Bransford, are they?"

"I suppose I wonder about the need you men find to compete, to try to win and be better than the rest. Is that not an odd way to express your allegiance to one another?"

"Ah, I see your point. But we have always worked to hone our skills at various endeavors. Through school, through the years of our friendship, competition has been basic to our attachment to one another. Immodest as it sounds, I was always the leader in the final standings. I would hate to see that change."

"Even with your . . ."

"Especially with my gamey leg. Now let me ask you, Miss Bransford. Is there not a hint of rivalry in the relations among ladies? Are you not looking for the newest fripperies, the prettiest gowns, the most flattering poses?"

"For most ladies, I am sure you are correct, Lord Matthew. As for me, I have never cared for that tussle."

"That is because you are gracious, generous, and

kind, my dear. If you were to deck yourself out in the latest modes, you would leave the competition far behind."

Her blush rebloomed. "What silly flattery! I lack almost every quality expected in a reigning beauty."

"Why, Miss Bransford, I would never have thought you were one to troll for compliments."

She ducked her head again, and he continued. "If I might be so bold, you have superior attributes in all regards. Your hair is lovely, highlighted in gold. Your brow is wide and smooth, your eyes the color of a sunny sky—"

Her head snapped up. "Stop! I have never heard anything so preposterous."

"You have a saucy streak, which is charmingly contrary to your angelic countenance. Your figure is perfect—"

"Please, Lord Matthew, you have quite sufficiently proved your command of flummery and nonsense."

He had never seen her so lovely, eyes flashing, almost shaking with indignation. "I mean every word I spoke."

"Fustian is what my mother would call it."

"But I am serious. Just as serious as I am when I say I intend to be the victor in our fishing competition. And, if you will excuse me, I also must return to the billiard room to defend my standing there."

He rose, lifted her hand to his lips, and bowed.

She stood. "Wait. Can you meet me in the stillroom, after luncheon?"

"I should be honored." He left the room, a spark of warmth growing in his heart.

* * *

When he was gone, Corey realized she had been holding her breath. She inhaled deeply and stared at the back of her hand where the touch of his lips still burned. As did the knee he touched ten minutes ago.

She felt the onset of tears and fought them back. Was there a single honest word among any he uttered? Certainly if he suspected she had strong feelings for him, he was being excessively cruel to tease her.

She sat down again and stared at the figurines, though her thoughts remained on Lord Matthew. His extravagant compliments aside, Corey had learned a great deal more about him. This series of contests was especially important to him. Probably because his wounded leg weakened his abilities and there would be nothing more in life he hated than to be weak. Except to be the object of pity. That would be worse. So everything he did here at Lodesham Hall was aimed at meeting the challenge, no matter how much pain it brought him.

His words of admiration to her were mere flattery. She would be a fool to assign more meaning there. But he might sincerely appreciate the mixture of herbs she had blended earlier.

After they ate, while she waited for Lord Matthew to come to the stillroom, she unscrewed the jar and sniffed the ointment she made for him. It smelled of rosemary and beeswax mixed with comfrey. Mrs. Newsome, Elaine's housekeeper, had been delighted to share her dried herbs and her receipts. Added to Corey's own knowledge, she thought they had come up with a useful blend for him to rub into his muscles and into the scars.

She replaced the lid and set the jar on the table.

When he entered, he was smiling and shaking his

head. "Seems that for all the time I once spent in this house, I have never had to find the stillroom, Miss Bransford. Fortunately, Oakley set me on the right course when I interrupted him polishing the silver."

"I would have brought this to you in the drawing room, but I thought perhaps you would not want to call the attention of your friends to . . ."

"Quite right. The less they notice my situation, the better. Now tell me, what is this and what do I do with it?"

"It is a blend of herbs known for their healing properties. It will not bring miracles, but I hope you will find it soothing. He stood close to her and took off the lid, holding it to his nose for a sniff, exactly as she had done moments ago. He inhaled deeply and she was pleased to see he did not wrinkle his nose in distaste.

"I do not recognize the fragrance."

"It is a combination of several herbs, most prominent is comfrey, known since the Middle Ages to bring comfort to injuries."

"So if I were a knight injured by that dragon, you would be the princess who ministered to my wounds."

She laughed lightly. "Yes, I suppose I would. Unless I was the village witch hiding in a little hovel mixing strange potions from secret recipes."

"You, a witch? Why, never, Cordelia, you who are the very epitome of maidenly beauty, the owner of that very countenance for which we knights venture forth on our quests."

"Kind sir, methinks your flattery is meant to turn my poor head."

"No, fair maiden, only meant to show the truth of it, for I know you are a princess in disguise. It is only for me to find the key to the sorcerer's spell over the kingdom to release you from your stillroom duties."

"The next time the children want a story told, I shall know to whom I should direct them! Lord Matthew, your imagination far outshines mine."

"Ah, do not try to fob me off, your highness. A royal princess with your obvious skills knows how to kindle magic in her mind's eye!"

She could only giggle, and thought how pitiful she must sound compared to his polished address, his clever words. She was suddenly tongue-tied, unable to carry her end of the little comedy. "I hope the balm will help."

He bowed and lifted her hand to his lips. "May I present the thanks of a grateful supplicant, your highness?"

Corey thought her heart might burst and she stammered an unintelligible reply, carried away by her growing awareness of his proximity, alone with her in the small room. He was only inches away, his hand warm, his lips softly brushing the back of her hand. Her knees felt like they had no ability to hold up her body. She grasped the edge of the table with one hand while the other tingled in reaction to his kiss.

When he closed the door behind him, she dropped onto a stool and held her head in her hands.

Why was she so overcome by his nonsense? He was only teasing her, the way an adult teased a child, the way a fine lord teased a village girl. She should not make anything of it beyond his natural flirtatiousness. To pretend his attentions to her could lead to anything more was to risk breaking her heart.

* * *

When Matt followed Perry, Cedric, and Alfred into
the Ivory Saloon to join the ladies after dinner, he was
charmed by the view of Cordelia sitting at the dainty
harpsichord in the corner of the room. She and
Elaine were playing little trills and chords in prepara-
tion, he hoped, for a musicale.

"How charming that you will play for us," Cedric
said, immediately going to the harpsichord. "May I
turn the pages for you?"

Miss Bransford shook her head. "There is no need.
I have known these tunes by heart since I was a child.
But thank you for asking."

Cedric shrugged and took a chair very close to the
players.

Matt sat on a brocade sofa, stretching his legs out before him. He was glad now, as the music began, he had
not gone upstairs to rub on more of Miss Bransford's
herbal ointment. It felt quite soothing and he had
almost left in order to shut himself away in his bedchamber where he could peel off his satin breeches and
prop up his leg while massaging in more of the balm.
But as he watched Miss Bransford play, he was very
pleased he was here instead. The leg could wait.

He remembered how pretty he thought she was five
years ago. When Perry had been determined to find
a wife, Matt had wondered why he chose Elaine over
Cordelia. They resembled one another, but Matt
found Cordelia's fair coloring more to his taste than
Elaine's darker hair and brows. Then there was the
matter of Elaine's family and their money, which the
Bransfords lacked. After Perry had made his choice
known, Cedric declared his interest in Cordelia, and
consigned Matt to the role of sporadic dancing partner
and occasional flirt. Miss Bransford had discouraged

Cedric and returned home to Yorkshire before the end of the Season.

Now she was as fresh and lovely as ever, with that captivating edge to her tongue that fascinated him. Most young ladies went out of their way to oblige and flatter, ending up saying nothing. Miss Bransford said what she thought, though most of the time she was sweet and generous. It appeared she saved her sharp rejoinders for the subject of men.

Lady Lodesham and Miss Bransford ended their sonatina with a flourish, met by applause. Matt joined in with enthusiasm. "Encore."

"P-please play more!" Alfred called.

"Yes, my dear." Perry wore a wide grin. "I have missed your playing lately. Please favor us with another."

Matt watched the ladies confer for a moment.

Elaine spoke for both of them. "We have not practiced this one, but we played it years ago. If we stumble, please bear with us."

Matt leaned back again and this time tried to listen to the notes. But his mind refused to concentrate on the music. Was Miss Bransford intolerant of all men? More probably of men like her brother. Matt knew George Bransford, who must have reached the age of thirty by now. George was a fellow of great pretensions and little patience, whether at university or at the gaming table. Miss Bransford could be forgiven her loathing of men like her brother. Did she classify the Quorn Quartet with George, as rattlepates and sapskulls?

What a lowering thought! But that very morning she had expressed her disapproval of the contests he engaged in. She had moderated her view a little when he explained, but she must know they bet on the results.

She would be naturally wary of anyone who wagered after the disastrous amounts her brother lost. Perry had reminded him a few minutes ago over their glasses of port about the disgrace that sent George abroad.

Matt again tried to concentrate on the music but could not help noticing the smirk on Cedric's face as he watched Cordelia. Yes, Matt thought, it was a good thing he stayed here. Miss Bransford might need a bit of protection from Cedric tonight.

This time when the music ended and the applause followed, Lady Lodesham declined their request to play again, even to repeat the sonatina. Instead, she suggested setting up a table for cards.

Miss Bransford's face fell. "Oh, I have not played in years. I do not even recall the names of the games!"

Perry stepped to her side. "Then you shall be my partner, Cordelia. I often confuse the rules of various games, so I prefer a cohort who is tolerant of my lapses."

Cedric took Corey's elbow and accompanied her to the card table. "And I shall be her tutor."

She gave a little curtsy. "Why, thank you, Mr. Williamson."

Matthew gritted his teeth. Cedric had outmaneuvered him to spend the evening at Cordelia's side. Now Matt was relegated to watching from afar as Alfred and Elaine took the chairs as a pair opposing Corey and Perry.

Cedric pulled a chair to Corey's elbow and sat beside her as Alfred dealt a game of whist. *Get out of there,* Matt wanted to snarl at Cedric. *Stop trying to peer down Miss Bransford's bodice!*

"Do you remember anything about the game, Corey?" Elaine asked.

"Not very much. I have not played for years."

Cedric adjusted his chair so he was practically on top of Corey. "I will help you, my dear."

Matt wanted to throttle him, but he had been slow off the mark. Cedric would be her instructor. Matt turned away and found a *Gentleman's Magazine* on a table, sitting by a lamp to flip through the pages.

A life of James I. A new translation of Ovid. A report on the British Museum. Since nothing caught his fancy, he walked across the room, taking care not to favor his weak leg, glancing into the little chamber where he had sat this morning with Miss Bransford. At the doors to the terrace, he opened one and peered outside. The rain had stopped and a few clouds chased across a moonlit sky. Tomorrow might be perfect for fishing.

Laughter came from the card table, and Matt winced at the sound of Miss Bransford joining in. He was beginning to care for her far too much, particularly if she disapproved of him. He had never been close to offering marriage to anyone, though he was not exactly opposed to the idea of having a family. He had a handsome estate in the West Country with an old house dating from the Jacobeans. With a little work, it would be ideal for a wife and children.

He glanced again at Miss Bransford, her brow furrowed in concentration as she pondered her choice of cards. Cedric leaned over her shoulder, touching her arm as he pointed at her hand. Matt wished he could box Cedric tonight. To put Cedric flat on his back, Matt would not need anywhere near the four minutes he had before his leg weakened. Matt forced himself to settle back on the sofa and thumb through the magazine again.

"Matt, will you take my hand?"

Perry's voice broke into Matt's attempt to focus on the agricultural reports. "Do you wish to quit playing?"

"We have only a few more hands, and I want to check the weather."

Matt took his place. "I have already looked and the stars are out."

"C-capital!" Alfred fanned his hand. "Tomorrow, the trout!"

Matt took Perry's chair, picked up his cards, and stole a look at the other side of the table. Cedric was wrapped around Cordelia like the crust on a strawberry pastry. His nose almost touched her cheek as he whispered to her. For the rest of the game, Matt kept his eyes on his cards or anywhere but across from him.

When, at last, Elaine called an end to the game, she pointed to the score pad. "You did very well, Corey. I think you remember everything. Even splitting the take with your partners, you have ended up with more than three guineas."

Cordelia gasped in surprise. "But we were not really playing for money, were we?"

Elaine gave a laugh. "Of course! We always want to make a game worth the attention of the gentlemen, you know."

Miss Bransford stood. "I had a fine tutor in Mr. Williamson. He deserves a share of the winnings."

Matt wanted to choke, but he noted with approval that she kept the chair between her and Cedric.

Cedric shook his head. "You were an apt pupil. I deserve nothing."

Lady Lodesham rang for the tea tray and moved to a sofa in the center of the room. The others followed and Matt watched Cedric take Cordelia's arm and attempt to steer her to a settee where he could sit beside her. To Matt's satisfaction, she chose a small chair instead.

When they each had their cup of tea in hand, Elaine called for silence. "Perry and I have decided to hold a little ball in two weeks. We will invite a few of our neighbors."

Matt stifled a frown. Dancing would not be the best thing for his leg. He glanced at Miss Bransford, for whom the announcement had obviously been an unwelcome surprise. Her face held a sort of glassy-eyed shock at the announcement, and she seemed entirely unaware that Cedric was leaning over her, whispering, apparently soliciting her promise of dance partnership already.

Why would a ball be so distasteful to Cordelia? As he recalled, she danced prettily enough. Even if she despised Cedric's attentions, nothing untoward could happen at a country house party of friends and neighbors.

Matt realized that Perry had addressed a question to him. "Sorry, I was already choosing my flies for tomorrow. What was it you asked?"

"Just that, Matt. After a rain like today's, the river might be a bit murky even after a quiet night."

Alfred came over and entered the discussion of strategies for outsmarting the trout. "I have a f-fly with a bit of silver thread that should attract the attention of the most sluggish fish."

A few moments later, when Matt glanced over at Corey's chair, he was surprised to find it empty. Neither she nor Cedric was any longer in the room.

Matt got to his feet. "Excuse me, I am going to take a look at those clouds and grab a breath of air."

The moonlight was intermittent as the clouds

scudded across the sky. But Matt saw Miss Bransford and Cedric only a few steps across the terrace. Her hand was pressed against his chest, holding him at arm's length. She shook her head from side to side in a classic negative stance.

Matt edged closer, staying in the shadows against the house. He felt his pulse quicken, his hands curl into fists. With just one more jot of provocation, he would plant Cedric a full-fledged facer.

Seven

"I have told you, Mr. Williamson. I have no intention of kissing you."

"You used to call me Cedric, Cordelia. And you used to like my kisses."

If she had not been so amazed at the sudden announcement of the upcoming ball, Corey would never have allowed herself to be entrapped into coming outside alone with him. "I remember only one attempted kiss. And I did not like it at all."

Cedric whispered to her. "Oh, come now, my dear. Admit the truth. You will remember if you give me just one little kiss."

Corey tightened her shawl around her shoulders against the chill of the night. "I am finding it rather damp out here, Mr. Williamson. I—"

She took a step back as Cedric came nearer.

"Now Corey, do not be unreasonable. I can easily teach you to enjoy a few kisses in the moonlight."

Corey wished she could shove him off the terrace into the shrubbery. "Look here, Cedric. I do not wish to hurt your feelings, but you are quickly extinguishing any positive memories I have of you by this constant quest for kisses. I find it excessively tiresome."

Cedric's move to embrace her was frozen by another voice, coming from the shadows.

"Lovely evening," Lord Matthew spoke in a casual drawl. "Hope those clouds are gone by mornin'. Fishin' should be capital!"

Cedric shrunk back and fingered the flower tucked in his lapel. "Surely will be, Matt. Now if you will excuse me, I shall make my good nights to our hosts and let Morpheus carry me off to dreamland." He bowed low and walked back into the house.

Corey drew a deep breath. "You do have a talent for appearing at opportune times, Lord Matthew."

"I hope I did not interrupt a tender moment."

She tossed her head. "Cedric has very strange ideas of what I would enjoy. No matter how many times I tell him no, he tries again and again."

"I was surprised a few moments ago when I looked up to find you both gone. If I may ask, why did you come out here alone with him if you were trying to discourage his, ah, his unwelcome advances?"

She looked out over the lawn where droplets of water glowed in the moonlight. "A fair question. I was not thinking. I was still trying to figure out why Elaine would announce a ball so suddenly. She said nothing to me about it earlier."

"Elaine must think you will enjoy the dancing."

Corey retightened her shawl. "I fear she had a different motive. If she had told me before she announced it to everyone, she knew I would object. Then, as the ideal hostess, she would have been obligated to cancel her plans. Elaine would never be rude enough to go against the wishes of a guest. But neither would I be impolite enough to find fault with her idea in the presence of her husband's visitors."

"And why would she think you might not care for a

ball? Ladies, in my experience, usually look forward to such an occasion."

"For some reason, I believe she thinks we should be acquainted with some of her neighbors." She would not go so far as to admit to Lord Matthew that Elaine must be trying to find her an eligible match. Corey even hated to admit it to herself.

But that was exactly what Elaine was up to with this sudden announcement of an entertainment for the nearby gentry. She had whispered to Corey that the invitations were already written.

Lord Matthew stood at some distance from her. Clouds blotted out the moon and in the dim light, she could barely see his face as he spoke.

"I know she does not entirely approve of the Quorn Quartet. Surely she would not be attempting to marry one of us to a local girl!"

Corey gave a little laugh. "Probably not. Unless she has a scheme to get even with you for interrupting her bridal trip. Perhaps she has a plan to abduct the next bridegroom."

He joined in her laughter. "Touché, Miss Bransford. I wondered if you knew of that, our most outrageous prank."

"Even today, Elly can hardly bring herself to voice her feelings about what you did. I do not think the word 'prank' would be the one she would choose to describe it."

"I am sure she has an extensive vocabulary of epithets for the three of us guilty parties."

"I should more likely characterize her view as rage beyond words."

"Well put. I wanted to speak with you in private for a moment to thank you for the ointment. It is indeed soothing in this wet weather, and I am eager to use it again when I prepare to retire."

In spite of the chill, Corey felt a warm flush of pleasure. "I am so pleased it has helped you. I will make up another batch for you soon."

"I would appreciate that very much. Now, we should not linger any longer out here in the damp. May I escort you indoors?"

Corey nodded and took his arm. But she rather wished he had stayed out with her and carried through on Cedric's lesson in kissing. With Lord Matthew, she might have enjoyed the experience.

For the next few days, the skies refused to cooperate with the plans for fishing, or anything else that required outdoor activity. The streams were murky with run-off, the lawns spongy with water, and even the gravel paths full of puddles.

Inside the house, the pervasive gloom was broken from time to time by one or another of the guests making a valiant effort to amuse the others, but generally, everyone was downcast and impatient.

Except Corey. She used the opportunity to work on her sewing projects and explore the nursery. As the days passed, the children became more comfortable with her and she with them. They liked to hear her stories, both the books she read to them and the ones she invented. Bundled against the weather, she managed one trip to play with the puppies and see their brother at Mrs. Hitchens's house. The baby was beginning to recognize all of them, or perhaps it was only his sunny disposition and her imagination combining in a fantasy world. She found she loved to sit on the bench at Mrs.

Hitchens's table and bounce him on her knee, a horsey ride that never failed to make him laugh out loud.

On several mornings, to defy the persistent rain, the men spent time working on the streams that led into the river, strategically placing rocks and woven willow traps to narrow the bed of the streams and make them run faster, multiplying the spots where the wily trout would like to rest and watch for the mayflies and other lures floating on the surface of the water. On those days, at luncheon, Corey was amused to hear their accounts of their soggy mornings, but she worried about what the activity cost Lord Matthew.

She thought about him while she worked in the stillroom in the afternoon. The pain of his wound must have been, must still be, excruciating. She wondered if she would have the nerve, the gumption, to act as he did, to force himself to push harder every day until it returned to the strength he desired. This strength was not the caprice of a childish person, but the determination of a strong, courageous man. He was not only fun-loving, but a person of more depth than she had suspected.

Her thinking had undergone a real change. While her opinion of Cedric continued to fall lower, her view of Matthew rose higher and higher. Where once she had admired him for his genial, if brief, attentions to her long ago, thinking of his attractive face and countenance, her feelings now went far beyond the superficial. A man who had the strength of character to persist after almost a year of pain and struggle had substance she never before suspected.

She made more of the balm for Lord Matthew and tried a receipt for another skin creme for Elaine.

On Friday morning, Corey placed the jar of creme

in her reticule and carried a hot teapot and cups on a
little tray to Elaine's boudoir. She tapped on the door
and opened it when Elaine bid her enter.

"How are you feeling this morning, cousin dearest?"

Elaine, propped against a pile of pillows and wearing
a lacy cap, gave a groan of misery. "As usual. The mere
thought of food is beyond endurance."

"I brought you a tisane to help your nausea."

"I will try anything."

Corey poured just half a cup and handed it to
Elaine. "This is very mild, brewed with camomile. If a
swallow goes down well, you can have more." She set
the tray on the dressing table, carefully pushing the
scent bottles aside.

Cautiously, Elaine sipped a little, then paused for a
few moments, peering into the liquid and then up at
Corey. She took another sip and held out the cup for
more. "This has very little taste, but the fragrance is
lovely. Where did you get it?"

"Your stillroom is well supplied with herbs and
essences of flowers. Mrs. Newsome was quite proud of
her jellies and her potions. I am surprised she has not
tried out a few on you, Elaine."

"She has, but however advantageous calfs-foot jelly
may be for good health, in my condition, I am not interested." Elaine finished the tea, leaned back against
the pillows, and closed her eyes.

Corey watched her cousin's face as her brow
smoothed out and a touch of pink colored her cheeks.
Corey poured more into the cup and carried it to the
bedside again. "Try another cup, then take a little rest.
I can bring you a cold compress for your forehead."

Elaine took the cup and drank. "I will rest in a moment." She set the half-full cup on a marble table at

her bedside. I need you to bring me two gowns from the armoire."

Corey shook her head. "When you have finished the tisane, I will rub this ointment onto your back. It will ease any pain you feel later and help you sleep."

Elaine shook her head. "That can wait. For the moment, my innards feel decent, and I need you to do me a favor."

"But—"

"How can you argue with a female in my circumstance, Corey?"

"All right, I can see it would be useless to argue. Now what is it you want?"

"In the armoire. There is an apricot gown and one of a silvery blue. Please bring them to me."

Corey did as she was told and draped the dresses over the edge of the bed.

Elaine nodded. "Now hold the blue one up to you, Corey."

Again, Corey followed directions and took the silky fabric off the hanger. She held it up to her shoulders and laughed at her reflection in the mirror. "It is missing the bodice, Elaine."

"Do not be a goose. It has plenty of bodice and look how perfectly the color complements your eyes. You must try it on, Corey."

"I could not, Elaine. I could never wear a dress like this." She fingered the filmy silk, as light and airy as feathers.

"You will look lovely in it. I insist you put it on." Elaine pulled a dainty handkerchief from under a pillow and touched it to the corners of her eyes as if she was weeping. "I insist."

Corey rolled her eyes, but she untied the tapes of

her gown and slipped it off. She started to put the gown over her shift, but Elaine stopped her.

"No! That gown was specially made with the under-garments built in. You must take off your shift."

Reluctantly, Corey stripped off the shift and dropped the gown over her head.

Elaine called for her maid. "Sawyer, see if you can lace up the back of Miss Bransford's gown."

When Sawyer successfully tightened the laces and fastened the hooks, Corey turned toward the mirror. The sleeves were made of silver tissue silk, as was the tiny bodice. She had never worn a dress with such a low neckline and she stared at herself for a moment in utter shock.

Elaine giggled. "I wish you would take a look at the expression on your face, Corey. You look like you are seeing an apparition!"

Corey was appalled at the amount of skin that swelled above the neckline. "This dress is all wrong for me. But it will look wonderful on you."

"Not any more. It looked perfect when I had my last fitting a few weeks ago, but now my bosom has en-larged. I will not be able to wear it. By the time I have my figure back, it will probably be out of date. So you must wear it to the ball."

"I cannot! I look like a wanton, positively indecent. I could not hold up my head."

"Do not be silly. It will be perfect when Sawyer takes a few tucks here and there."

"But you cannot give me a gown you have never worn! That is ridiculous."

Elaine finished her tea and gave Corey a wink. "I certainly can. I have more gowns than I will ever need. Sawyer, where is that apricot muslin that makes my complexion sallow? If it is flattering to you, Corey, you may as well take it. I will never wear it."

Sawyer unlaced the back of the silvery blue gown and lifted it over Corey's head. She could not resist letting the silken fabric slide through her fingers again. Perhaps she could make it work but even with a few tucks, it would need something to fill in the décolletage.

When Sawyer helped her into the second gown, she immediately admired the shade, more of a light orange than apricot, to her way of thinking. But with the world of fashion being so mired in overdone rhetoric, she was surprised the color was not called something even more exotic like Persian Apricot Spice or Essence of Tangerine. The color did go well with her honey tresses and blue eyes, making her skin glow.

Elaine approved. "Yes! That is what apricot can do for the right skin tone. I should never have allowed Madame Kuony to talk me into purchasing that muslin. But on you, it is lovely."

Corey could not help but agree, nodding her head. "If I accept your generosity and take this gown, you can keep the silver-blue. I will save this for the ball." Corey put on her shift and the old sprigged muslin she'd had for at least three years.

"Never! That is a day dress and you cannot dress it up enough to make it suitable for evenings. I insist that you wear the silver-blue to the ball. Now, Sawyer, take the apricot to Miss Bransford's clothes press and see what you can do about making the silver bodice fit her."

The maid draped both gowns over her arm and left.

"Are you quite sure you are up to having this ball, Elaine? I do not mean to be unappreciative, but I do not understand why you are putting yourself to all this trouble."

"To be honest, I enjoy dancing. As you know, I am a shallow, selfish creature, and I am thinking of my own pleasure. In a few months I will be waddling around with a figure the shape of the dovecote. No dancing then."

"Do not give me that nonsense, Elaine, you fraud! You just gave me two lovely gowns and you say you are selfish. As for being shallow, do not suppose I will accept that drivel! Unless I am quite mistaken, cousin dear, all of this is an elaborate ruse to find me a husband. I see through your ploy to your true motives."

Elaine sank back into the pillows. "What tarradiddle you speak. Now go away and let me rest." She closed her eyes and sighed.

Corey picked up her tray and crossed the room. "Sleep well, dearest. I will take this up with you later. As she pulled the door shut she heard the unmistakable thump of a pillow hitting its other side.

One dreary afternoon, Corey sat before the bookcase in the nursery and hunted through the jumble of books. Far back on the shelf, behind *The Butterfly's Ball* and *The Grasshopper's Feast,* she spied the worn blue binding of *Ancient Tales of English Heroes.*

She clutched the book to her, arms wrapped around it protectively. She felt as though she had found a little piece of her childhood, evidence her life had once been perfect, just as she remembered. She had adored her older brother George, who was always into mischief, but never seriously so until he left for university. Or so it seemed to her. He was a bruising rider, and she worked hard to keep up, putting her far ahead of the other girls she knew. Until Georgie's debts piled up, her family had been comfortable, well-off if not wealthy. They had their spacious vicarage with many servants along with ample means for a genteel and comfortable life.

Corey tried to shake off the memories of how those privileges disappeared. More than the loss of the material goods, she remembered her mother weeping, her father grim-faced. A feeling of sadness pervaded their home, made worse by the occasional periods of hope when Georgie bragged about some great accomplishment he was about to achieve. Then, when he was accused of cheating at cards, there was no other recourse but to provide the means to send him abroad once the scandal was smoothed over and his debts discharged. Of course, as always, he promised he would come about, that everything would be fine in the end.

But even if he did manage to make his own way eventually without support from his father, Georgie could never restore his mother's good health by pretending her years of worry and strain did not exist. Nor could her father ever repossess the years of disappointment, the desolation of having an only son prove worthless.

"Read us a story, Corey?" Henry left his blocks and looked at her expectantly. She called to Gina, and for the next half hour, read the story of St. George, one they heard before but like all children, seemed to enjoy again and again. To Corey it was that delightful window to her early years for which she had longed. Both the words and the pictures were enchanting.

When the story was concluded and Bess had taken

the children off to luncheon, Corey knew she had to find Lord Matthew to show him the book.

Matt sat with Perry, Alfred, and Cedric in the breakfast room. On the table they had assembled an amazing array of tools, thread and string, bits of colored fabric and oiled paper, fishhooks of many sizes, and feathers in a heap that looked as though someone had sneaked around the estate, plucking at the tails of unwary fowl or sleeping birds. Each man had a pad of green cloth before him where the result of the morning's exertions lay for comparison and model duplication.

Matt had his own theories and suppositions about what attracted trout to snap at a simulated insect. A touch of silvery material that flashed in the sun was his favorite addition to the feathers masking the hooks. Neither too large nor too small. Light enough to sail through the air with ease. Heavy enough to land with a gentle *plop* that stirred the water neither too much nor too little. A delicate balance that required a deft hand to tie the fly and to place it exactly where the trout would be uncontrollably tempted.

He chose another hook, a large one, perhaps suitable for that mean old trout they'd tried to snag for years. As he sorted through the feathers, looking for one that was the perfect size, he caught a movement out of the corner of his eye. He looked up and saw Miss Bransford peeking around the edge of the doorway, beckoning to him. He looked at the others, all bent over their work and listening to some story from Cedric to which he had stopped paying attention.

He looked back at Corey and gave a little nod. What could she be up to? he wondered. Whatever it was, it was a welcome reprieve from more of Williamson's boasting. Any attention from Cordelia was more than welcome!

He set the hook back in the box. "Guess I'll grab a breath of air before we eat."

Corey lurked around the corner, waiting for him.

"Thank you for getting up, Lord Matthew. I hate to disturb you, but I found that book we talked about. *Ancient Tales of English Heroes.*"

When they were seated in the morning room, Corey handed him the book.

"I remember it perfectly! Looking at this cover makes me feel about six years old again."

"I felt the same as I opened it. And when I saw the engravings . . ."

He leafed through the pages and found the story of St. George illustrated by an elaborate engraving of the dragon. He slowly shook his head, as if in wonderment. "It is just as I remember—the rearing horse, the helmet visor covering the saint's face. Those immense, pointed scales on the dragon's back and its three heads, all breathing smoke and fire. But do I not recall it was in color. I thought the dragon was green, the banner red and white, the sky blue."

"You may have had an edition in which the pictures had been colored. I remember it exactly this way, without embellishment. But I have seen many children's books in which the engravings are painted with watercolors."

He grinned and gave a little shrug. "Or perhaps I am letting my imagination run away with me. I have not looked at a child's book for at least fifteen years, I presume. Depending on the reliability of my recollections would be a distinct mistake, you know, Miss Bransford."

"Did you have a governess who read to you, Lord Matthew?"

"My brother and I shared a poor, harassed woman with my sisters until we were taken over by a tutor, equally harassed but far less strict."

He had not answered her question, but she did not want to pry further. It was just that she liked the thought of him as a little boy sitting under a tree, listening to this story. She was curious about who might have been reading.

He took out his pocket watch and checked the time. "After luncheon, perhaps you would like to accompany me to Dorchester. The rain is over, but the streams are too riled up for successful fishing. My grays need to stretch their legs and I thought we might have a look in the shops for a sailing boat for Henry to try on that duck pond."

"I should be most happy to accompany you, Lord Matthew. I might even pick up a few things at the draper's."

Silently she chastised herself. The prick of anticipation she felt seemed all out of proportion to the opportunity to buy a scrap of fabric or a packet of pins.

In the busy yard of the King's Arms, Matt left his tiger to see to the curricle and the pair of grays. He had already noted the high color on Cordelia's cheeks as they passed the cluster of shops on High East Street and he offered her his arm to go in search of a purveyor of children's toys.

The toy store was small and crammed with goods of all kinds. Two ladies and a gentleman occupied the proprietor, allowing Matt and Corey to look around at their leisure. Matt immediately spied a line of sailing boats in assorted sizes and styles placed on high shelves around the perimeter of the tiny shop. For the moment, until the proprietor was free and brought out a ladder, he could only look from a distance. Several met his criteria: good size but not too large for Henry to carry, one or two sails at the most for ease of operation. The scale models of ships of the line might be perfect for the mantel of an aspiring admiral, but they were much too complicated for a young boy.

Matt watched Cordelia admire the selection of dolls that filled several shelves. He had no idea there could be so many dolls of various sizes and shapes, from babies wrapped in flannel to elegantly dressed ladies complete with feathers on their hats.

"Do you see something you think Gina would like?"

"I am sure she would love any of these, but to tell the truth, they are more suited for an older girl. Gina sometimes drags her doll around by one leg with its hair trailing in the dust, so I think she is still too young for one of these lovely specimens."

"Are they fragile?"

"I would suspect so. I will find her something less easily broken."

Together they looked at balls, tops, blocks, and games. A set of checkers made Matt think of his games with his brother, and even with one of his sisters. There were small chess sets as well, but Matt followed Corey's example. Little Henry was still too young for chess.

Pairs of stilts brought him another flash of memory from childhood. "Did you ever try stilts, Miss Bransford?"

"I did not, but I think my brother did, and skinned

his knees so badly my father banished the stilts before I got a chance to try them. I imagine you were quite good at stilt-walking, Lord Matthew."

"As I recall, one of the tenants made me a pair, and I walked on them for weeks, or perhaps it was only a few days before I overstretched my abilities and suffered the same fate as your brother. My mother was particularly upset, as I recall, because my clumsy spill was right in the middle of the chicken yard. I managed to carry the odor of those fowl right into the house, all over my clothes."

He was delighted to see her laughter. "Your mama had a right to be disturbed. Whatever were you doing in the chicken yard, chasing the hens?"

"I loved to hear them cackle."

She gave a little shake of her head, then looked up at him with a smile. "Oh, here is Noah's Ark."

The large boat had a huge collection of carved animals both inside and next to it on the shelf, all colorfully painted and neatly placed in pairs. It reminded Matt of a much smaller version in his nursery. "The lions were my favorites long ago. Did you have an ark?"

"Oh, yes. Mine had only familiar animals like cows and pigs, however. Nothing exotic like giraffes or lions."

Her eyes lit up when she noticed a music box.

He opened the lid and listened to the tune. "If you buy this for Gina, I could buy Henry one of those drums to accompany her."

"Then Elaine would banish you forever. I do not think she wants to encourage Henry to march about the house banging on a drum."

"I am sure you are correct. The drum will stay here

in the shop. But I am sure both Gina and her mother will love the music box."

The proprietor, having finished with his other customers, hurried over. "May I assist you, my lord?"

"Yes. I am interested in one of those boats, one that will sail on a large pond for a boy of four or five."

The man moved a ladder into place and handed down two of the boats from the display. "Either of these would be suitable for a lad of that age. Both are well balanced and sturdy."

Matt examined them carefully. "I like the larger one. And I even like the little name tag, Zephyr."

While the proprietor wrapped the boat and the music box, Matt looked at a large display case of toy soldiers. From knights in armor to kilted highlanders, the assortment covered the centuries.

The proprietor came over to open the case. He removed a small figure. "Here is one of the latest we have, my lord. Just as they appeared at the glorious victory at Waterloo."

The sight of the soldier suddenly clogged Matt's throat and almost drove the breath from his chest. It wore his exact uniform, correct to the precise shade of the coat's facings.

He swallowed quickly and shook his head as if to clear it. "Very fine." His voice sounded like a croak.

He took the soldier from the man and held it for a moment before replacing it beside a mounted Hussar, also just as one would have appeared on the day of the battle.

He could not help the visions that filled his head, visions of that terrible day and how one of his proudest accomplishments had been to save his horse, his precious Zeus. Weak from loss of blood, he had searched the battlefield with the help of one of his sergeants. So many horses had died; he could remember the cries of the horses as vividly as those of the men. Long after they should have given up, he and Blake were exhausted and weak from loss of blood when a man rode up and there was Zeus, unmistakable with his crooked blaze and one white rim above his off-front hoof. At first the rider had been unwilling to surrender the horse but Blake talked him into it. Later when he was alone, Matt remembered sobbing with relief.

He shook himself back to the present. Corey looked at him quizzically. He managed a smile and stepped back from the case. "You have a very fine selection, sir."

He took the packages and returned the proprietor's bow with a nod as the man held open the door.

He took a deep breath. "I believe you had another visit to make, Miss Bransford?"

"Yes. May I meet you at the inn in a half-hour?"

"That should do nicely." He watched her make her way through the other shoppers and turn in a few doors down the street.

He turned back to the inn and forced each foot to follow the other until he reached the curricle and left the packages with his man. He had never needed a glass of spirits more!

Corey made her selections and hurried back to the inn as fast as she could. Matt's reaction to that toy soldier worried her. The color had drained from his face and he had stood as if in a trance for several moments.

She found him in a private parlor in the King's Arms, gazing into a mug of ale. She sat across from him at the table and touched his arm.

He looked up, obviously not having heard her enter.

"Lord Matthew, you have suffered for a very long time. Is your leg bothering you especially badly today?"

"What? Oh, yes. I mean, no. It is not bad, not really."

"I am afraid I find it hard to believe you. How were you wounded, if I may ask a touchy question? I believe you said it was in the battle?"

Eight

Matt stared into the distance, his ale forgotten. "Yes, at Waterloo, late in the day."

"How did you come to serve there?" Corey kept her voice low, hoping he would stop keeping his memories bottled up inside him.

He shrugged, then gave a rueful laugh. "After Napoleon turned up again, I volunteered. It was a foolish whim. I was too inexperienced."

"But had you not served in the army before?"

With a dismissive snort, Matt shook his head. "My experience was minimal. I spent most of the war years drilling militia and never had service abroad. I should have stayed home and minded my own business."

How true that was, he thought. But why had he said it to her? He would never have admitted inexperience to Perry or Cedric. He might have known how to order men to line up and present arms, though for the most part, they had only rakes and sticks, not muskets. In truth, he had no experience at all of the heat of battle, with the infernal noise, the rockets exploding, the fear twisting in his gut, the pounding of his pulse. The heart-stopping panic had almost overwhelmed him.

Matt felt cold perspiration break out on his back, his forehead. He lifted his fingers to wipe away the sweat, saw how his hand shook, and quickly thrust it behind him. He clenched his teeth and stared into the distance, covering his gulp of fear with a cough.

"You—" His voice croaked with tension and he coughed again. "You do not want to hear about the battle, Miss Bransford. War is a nasty thing."

He stole a look at her and saw that she stared down at her own hands twisting together. She must have seen the pain in his eyes and averted hers. He felt his face redden in embarrassment. How had he allowed himself to be so weak?

She raised her head but kept her eyes from his, gazing at the stream. "Yes, a nasty business, but not a topic unfit for my ears, Lord Matthew. I believe that those of us who remain ignorant will never understand. And, I wish to understand, I really do."

He drew a deep breath, shuddering a bit as he attempted to calm himself and drive away the demons. But they only attacked with more force. "The noise. The confusion," he muttered, then stopped himself. "You see, nothing prepares one."

"Go on, please."

"I had heard the tales but until you are there . . . Until you are there, you do not understand."

"I am trying."

Matt held up a hand as if to halt her. "No, it is not a fit subject for you."

"But I want to know more. Every person in the realm should hear about it."

He could not prevent the visions that filled his head. The man exploding before his eyes, spraying blood and brains all over him, over the men beside him. Only a few inches and he would have been there himself, splattered all over his men. The cannons resounded in his skull, the slippery, blood-soaked mud, the trampled ground strewn with bodies. He could not stop the shiver that shook him.

Corey touched his arm, then drew back her hand. "How were you wounded? Was it early in the battle?"

He summoned his normal tone, but when he spoke his voice sounded far away, shaky and tremulous. "I lost track of all time. With each charge of the enemy, we thrust them back. We had a superhuman energy, and each time we fought them off, they seemed to return in force. Again and again the waves of the enemy came, and each time men fell."

How sterile it sounded, this account. His words made it seem orderly and tidy, neatly organized, when, in fact, all was chaos and turmoil and misery. "They came and came again, then again. All day it continued."

"But you prevailed."

"Barely. The bravery was astonishing." Yes, bravery, though he had not felt the slightest bit courageous at the time. He was running on panic, he was pushing the men, screaming at them to reform their ranks. To reload, to stand, to bring up more ammunition. To reposition the artillery. To ignore the fallen beside them. By the time his leg crumpled beneath him, he was so covered in blood he knew not where the bullet had struck.

"It was late in the day when I took a hit. I did not know we had prevailed until the next dawn."

He stole a look at her face.

The tears ran down her cheeks.

Matt ran his fingers through his hair. "Forgive me. I should never have allowed myself . . ."

"But I begged you to continue." Her voice strangled

in her throat. "You warned me. You warned me more than once."

He felt as though he had violated some sacred trust, a kind of bond the men had among themselves. "I am sorry. I should not have listened to your pleas. Forgive me."

No one who had not been there could ever understand and he had made a fool of himself. Why had he allowed those awful thoughts to invade his brain, swirl around and leave him limp with their intensity?

The sum of his words moved her less than the emotions on his face, the rigid tension of his body, the shudder of his shoulders. In his eyes she saw his agony, though she knew it was only a glimpse. His deeper thoughts would forever haunt him.

She felt the strongest urge to smooth his hair, brush the wrinkles from his brow, press herself to his chest to dull the pounding of his heart. She moved around the table and sat beside him, wrapping her arms around him and clasping him close. She stroked his back and willed him to forget, to blot out the dreadful images that shook him.

He slipped his arms around her. Warmth suffused her chest, her lower regions. She wanted to take his evil thoughts as her own. She wanted to draw out his dreadful memories and send them flying away, never to return. She had made him lose control and for a man like Lord Matthew, that was a cardinal sin, the worst thing he could do. To drive away his cool demeanor and leave him a quivering child was wrong.

She did not know how long they clung together but

his jacket was wet with her tears when they finally pulled apart.

Corey found her voice at last. "I am the one who must apologize. I should not have urged you to think back on those dreadful times. I am very sorry. It was thoughtless of me to bring back all your worst feelings. But I do thank you nonetheless."

"You must not weep, Corey. Please do not weep." He stood and took an unsteady step away.

"It was wrong of me to make you recall those times. Very wrong." She took out a handkerchief and wiped her eyes.

He drew a deep breath and squared his shoulders. "I believe we should head back to Lodesham Hall."

She gave him a bright smile. "Yes, I believe we should."

Just past sunrise the next morning, the cool air was still damp from the previous day's rain. The birds were restless, swooping low in the misty air over the water, seeking the newly hatched mayflies. Beneath the surface of the streams, the trout lurked in the weeds, waiting for the insects to come within range of their greedy jaws.

Matt and Perry chose a stretch of the river's feeder stream at least a quarter-mile from Cedric and Alfred. Now that the time was here, Matt was impatient to begin. Standing on his bad leg might not be easy, but there was little in the world he enjoyed more than casting flies over the surface of the water, aiming for the hidey-holes the trout favored.

He unfolded the leather case in which he stored the flies and chose one from the several dozen he had tied. He blew gently on it to fluff up the bits of feather beside the hook, then fastened it to his line. His pole was made of ash, new two years ago, before he had gone with Wellington. The war had seemed over then, and selecting a new rod had been a pleasure, the promise of many enjoyable hours ahead. He had used it only a few times in the streams of Somerset near his own estate. That same year he had stocked the streams, and in another year at this time, the fish ought to be well-grown and ready for combat.

He watched Perry wade in a few yards upstream and cast his line toward the far bank where the water was deeper. His fly lit on the fast-running surface and it drifted downward without disturbance. No strikes. Too bad.

Matt stepped into the shallows and cast upward, letting the fly float down and past him. A shadow moved toward it, or was that his imagination? He reeled in the line and cast again in the same pattern. Again he thought he saw movement below the surface of the water but could not be certain. A third cast, then a fourth. Abruptly the line jerked and the pole bent almost double. His heart thumped as he watched for the crucial moment, then set the hook with a sharp jerk. He let out more line and reeled it in, playing the fish back and forth, hoping the line would not snag on a sunken limb. He whistled softly to Perry, who soon came beside him with a large net. For endless minutes, the fish ran, slowed, then ran again, once or twice breaking the surface of the water with a splash. The trout was slow to tire, slower than his own leg, but any thought of giving up was intolerable.

At last the fish seemed to have run out of energy,

and as Matt reeled him closer, Perry swept down with the net and captured the trout.

There was nothing more beautiful, Matt thought, than a glistening brown trout, just out of the water, its iridescent scales reflecting the early morning sun like a prism. He grasped the fish by its gills and lifted it from the net, twisting out the hook. Perry wrote the time in his notebook, then measured the trout's length. Matt hung it from a spring-like apparatus designed to give an approximate weight. Two and a half pounds, Perry wrote.

After one last admiring look, Matt gently lowered the trout into the water. With a swish of its tail, it disappeared into the depths. "Grow another pound or two, my friend, and perhaps we shall meet again in the future."

Perry slapped Matt's shoulder. "I feel sure you will win that wager on who caught the first one. I checked my timepiece with Cedric's a while ago, so we will know later what time he or Alfred hooked one."

"If I know Alfred, he is still trying to choose which fly to begin with. But then, did I not always manage to hook the first?"

"Yes, you usually had the first. And probably the largest and the last catch as well."

They kept their voices low, for legend had it that the trout listened in on human conversation and would quickly find new territory if anglers began to brag about their accomplishments.

Matt felt a patina of satisfaction settle over him. The first catch was always a thrill. He changed the fly to another version with slightly longer feathers and moved a few yards farther downstream to begin his new casts.

* * *

Corey was obligated to promise the creation of another new dress for Gina's doll before the little girl would stop fussing over staying behind. Henry had not the slightest compassion for his sister.

"She always cries when she does not get her way. Even Mama says so."

Corey took his hand in hers as they went down the staircase. "Gina is disappointed. You would be disappointed if I took her to watch the fishing and left you behind, Henry."

He pulled his hand away. "I would not cry like a baby."

"Of course you would not. You are older than Gina. She is only three years of age."

"She should not cry so much." His voice had the tinge of stubbornness she had heard in Perry's from time to time.

They took the basket cart to a little glen not far from the river, then climbed down and left the groom to watch Tommy, who hungrily dropped his muzzle to the succulent, long grass.

Corey held out her hand and Henry reluctantly took it. "I hope the fish are as hungry as Tommy."

Henry twisted his head to give the old pony a glance. "Tommy is always ready to eat. That is why he is so fat."

"Remember what Papa said, Henry. We must whisper as we get close to the stream."

The boy nodded, as if he did not trust his voice in a whisper. They first came upon Perry, who waved at them between casts. They stood near the bank of the stream, and Henry's eyes grew wide, watching his father expertly place his lure near the far edge of the stream, then allow it to glide with the current. Before long a fish broke the water and the fly disappeared. Perry set the hook with a jerk of his rod, then let the line sing out as the fish struggled to get away.

Corey watched the excitement on Henry's face as he danced from one foot to the other. "Come on, Papa." He looked stricken and lowered his voice to a near-whisper. "I am sorry."

"Do not worry, son. This trout's struggles have alerted all his friends to trouble. We can talk without doing any harm."

They watched Perry wrestle the fish for several minutes. Corey knew she was as wide-eyed as Henry watching her first fly-fishing fight. Matt came up the other bank holding a net on a long handle, and in moments, as Perry reeled, he dipped the net into the water and came up with the fish.

Henry squealed his pleasure. "Papa, Papa!"

Corey kept her distance, but Henry ran right up to inspect the fish. Even from a distance, Corey had to admire the color of the fish, a deep brown on its back, shading to cream on its stomach, decorated with black spots and flecks of red and coral. The men measured the fish, jotted down its weight, and released it back into the water.

Henry did not approve. "Papa, you let it go. After you caught it, you should keep it."

Perry gave his son an affectionate pat on the head. "My boy, we keep only a few. We put them back to catch again another day. The sport, you see, is more important than the take. Someday, you will understand."

"But he was a big 'un."

"Barely two pounds. He has some growing to do.

Now, come with me and we'll find a quiet pool down the river and I'll let you try your hand at still fishing. We'll be back in an hour, Miss Bransford. I leave you to watch Matt catch at least a dozen more trout."

When Perry and Henry disappeared around the bend, Matt put the measuring tape back in a basket and spread a rug on a fallen log. "If you will take a seat, I will be gratified to take my weight off my leg."

She sat at one edge of the rug, arranging her skirts to keep them from dragging in the weeds.

He enjoyed the brief glimpse of her ankles.

"Does it ache dreadfully, Lord Matthew?"

"Please, while we are in the midst of the wilderness, call me Matt. Formality seems out of place out here, do you not agree, Cordelia?"

"Indeed, and you may address me as Corey, if you wish. Cordelia is rather a mouthful, I think."

"Very good, Corey."

The tone of his deep voice and the smile on his lips just a foot or two away gave her pulse a little jolt. To cover her loss of composure, she stammered witlessly. "I-I was surprised to see you l-let the fish go, ah, Matt."

He seemed not to notice. "We keep few of them. They are not particularly tasty, you know. Some of their cousins are much more savory, and Perry's chef rolls his eyes if we bring him more than three or four of the browns. Some of the grooms enjoy them, probably because they grew up with stolen brown trout on their home tables."

Corey was doubly surprised. "You mean the local people poach fish from Perry's streams?"

"Fish, birds, and hares, too, from time to time, I imagine. It is said some men can catch trout with their hands. Others build traps of saplings. Perry's agent fines them if he catches them, but no one worries too much. The same thing happens at my place in Somerset. A bit of poaching is tolerable, though I would never let my tenants hear me say so."

"Where is your estate, Matt?"

"In Somersetshire, not far from Wells. Have you ever been in that region?"

"I am afraid not. I have not traveled much."

"It is pretty country. The trout are not as numerous as here in the chalk streams, but there are enough. Now if you will come close to the bank, I will give you a little lesson in fly casting, an ancient art in this part of the country."

She stood beside him while he explained how to hold the pole in one hand and the line in the other, to flip it back and then forward with a quick movement of the arm, but even more with a flick of the wrist. He demonstrated the action, which placed the fly on the surface of the water, falling neither too hard nor too lightly. She had watched when he and Perry cast, and the feat was smooth, appeared effortless, seemed a simple matter. The flies landed just right, exactly where they were meant to go.

When he handed her the pole, she tried to imitate his movement, but the fly went all awry, caught in a branch. He unhooked it, and she tried again, less vigorously. It hardly moved. Again she tried, and it flopped uselessly.

"I do not seem to have the knack for it," she said.

"Here, let me try to show you." He stood behind her and stretched one arm along hers that held the pole. The other hand he wrapped around hers holding the line. His chest was pressed firmly against her back and the sensations that sped through her wiped out any interest she had in properly casting the fly, much less in hooking a trout.

His head was just above hers, his mouth almost at her ear. "Here," he said, "let us try again." He pulled her arm back a little, then pressed it forward, flexing his wrist with hers. The lure flew through the air and landed in the stream.

"Much better, Corey!"

"Quite so!"

With his other hand he helped her pull on the line so that the fly skittered across the water before she reeled it in. Again they repeated the action, and once more. Despite her obsession with his arms on hers, his chest rubbing at her back, Corey thought she began to get the feel of a proper cast. He helped her once more, then stood back.

"Try it on your own."

She attempted to concentrate and managed to land the fly on the water, though not near her target.

He stepped to her again and wrapped his arms around her once more. "Let's try again. I do not wish to stop."

He put into words her exact feelings. How nice it was, how good it felt to have his arms around her, to be so close. Every time he spoke, his breath ruffled her hair. When he breathed, she felt the intake of air. His arm rested on hers, the two moving as one, a magical touch she had never before known.

She turned her head to look back at him. There were words she wished to say, but none formed in her throat. She felt lightheaded. His lips were so near.

The moment seemed to last forever before they heard the returning voices of Perry and Henry, and pulled apart. He took the fishing pole from her and smiled down into her face. "A most satisfying lesson, Cordelia." His voice was a husky whisper.

She tried again to speak, to agree. But once more, words failed her. All she could feel was the loss of his embrace and it made her tremble.

Hours later, Corey still felt the tingle of his arms. When she returned to the Hall with Henry, she went to her bedchamber and sank into a chair. The man who told her of his experience at Waterloo yesterday was a very different man from the charming Lord Matthew of today. He changed from poignant to seductive, and both guises sent her emotions whirling.

There was also the Matthew who was a comrade in the reckless pranks of Perry, Cedric, and Alfred. But at the battle, instead of an imprudent and irresponsible rake, Matt had been conscientious to his duty, stunned by the carnage around him, steadfast and resolute, qualities she never suspected he had. And to think she had once guessed his bad leg was the result of a drunken fall!

It must have been an effort for him to return to that teasing charm when he stood behind her and tried to help her learn the combination of arm motion and flick of the wrist that sent the fly arcing into the water. She sank back in the chair and tried to push away the memories of their bodies pressed together. His hand on hers, his arm guiding hers, his chest rubbing against her back . . .

She jumped in surprise at a tapping on her door. "Yes," she called.

Fanny came in with a little curtsy. "Her ladyship asks you come to her, if you can, miss."

"Now?"

"Yes'm. She is in a state, miss."

"Thank you, Fanny." Corey did not wait to brush her hair, but hastened to Elaine's boudoir.

Instead of being in bed, as Corey had feared, Elaine was pacing back and forth in her boudoir, waving a letter in one hand and muttering to herself.

"Elly, what has happened?"

Elaine whirled and shook the letter at Corey. "Simply the worst, the most terrible thing. Perry's dreadful mama will be here tomorrow! It is more than I can bear."

Corey was not sure she understood. "The dowager? Coming here?"

"Yes. Lady Lodesham and Perry's sister Sophronia are staying the night at Elmbrook, just a few miles away. They arrive at the Hall tomorrow in time for luncheon."

"Is Perry aware of—"

"For all I know, he instigated the whole thing. We have already sent the cards for our ball next week and cannot cancel. She will ruin everything, telling one and all how foolish I am to have so many children so quickly. She will do her best to make me the laughing-stock of the county."

"But Perry—"

"He is trying to marry off his sister, just as the dowager is. With three single males here, what better way to catch one than to have her on hand? But he does not realize how the dowager poisons those men against Sophy."

"What do you mean?"

"Most men believe daughters turn out much like their mothers. After a few days in the dowager's company, neither Matt nor Cedric nor Alfred will have the slightest interest in Perry's sister."

"But what is—"

"The dowager is imperious, haughty, and thoroughly unpleasant. She seems to believe it is her privilege as an older woman to tell everyone else exactly what to do, how to do it, and then supervise their execution of her orders. To men other than Perry, I expect she is a terror."

"Surely she will be glad of another grandchild . . ."

"Oh, Corey, did you not hear what I said? After Gina, she told me to avoid Perry for at least a year. She practically suggested I send him off to an opera dancer! She thinks children should be spaced two years apart. She rebuked me for ignoring her advice before Lawrence, and she will be livid that I have ignored her again."

"Perhaps she will not know—"

"Oh, I am certain she knows already. She has an appalling companion who wrings every bit of gossip out of the servants. I have often suspected she puts them on the rack! The dowager is blind as a bat, but Ingrey misses nothing. Can you imagine? The dowager even insists that I call her 'Mama.' It seems an insult to the memory of my own dear mother. As for the baby on the way, I am sure the Quartet members already know. Either Perry has told them, or they see how peckish I am and draw their own conclusions. I assume they have already entered their bets on the child's gender and arrival date. They bet on everything else."

"Surely they would not wager on such a—"

"They not only have bets on fish and horses and their boxing matches. Corey, they have even bet on you."

"On me?"

"Cedric has put money on being able to kiss you."

"They have wagered on what?" Corey felt a buzzing in her ears, a heavy weight pressing her neck. She sat down abruptly.

Elaine held up one hand, as if that might calm Corey's temper. "I went to Perry's desk while he was fishing this morning. I read their betting book. They are betting on whether Cedric can . . . ah, if Cedric will be able to earn your . . . your kisses."

"Ha! Not whether he will able to compromise me in the shrubbery for a lark? I suspect you are being far too circumspect, Elly. How dare they use me so!"

"I am not sure they mean for Cedric to trifle with your affections. I am sure they do not want to hurt you."

"Oh, do not be a goose, Elly. It is their care-for-nothing irresponsibility. They would not care if they hurt me. Look what they did to you and Perry."

"That was five years ago. But never mind that non-sense. What am I to do about the dowager?"

Elaine was too distraught to go down for dinner, but Corey decided to meet the men in the drawing room before she had her meal served in her bedchamber.

When she entered, Perry led the way in bowing to her but she wasted no time on niceties. "I wish to join in the wager you have made on Cedric's ability to bring me to *point non plus*."

In unison, the jaws dropped on all four faces.

"What?"

"Huh?"

"You do?"

"The d-devil!"

The utterances melded together in a brief chorus that made Corey grin.

The value of shock!

She looked from face to face. At the moment, not even Lord Matthew's smile moved her. "Now that I have earned a few coins at the card table, I wish to expand my gaming experience."

Cedric took a step toward her, sputtering. "But you . . . your . . . your actions will decide the result of the wager . . . you cannot . . ." He stopped speaking and shrugged his shoulders.

"I thought the wager centered on *your* behavior, Mr. Williamson. Are not your talents, your charm, and seductive powers at issue?"

"But . . . but . . ." Cedric shifted from one foot to the other, apparently unable to sort out his thoughts.

Corey glanced at the other three men, who grinned and elbowed each other. "I have three guineas I wish to bet on my capacity to resist Cedric's charms."

They looked at one another without speaking.

She stared at each one in turn. "Will you not allow me to join in the wager?"

Cedric threw up his hands as if surrendering.

She pressed on. "Gentlemen, will you get out the betting book and allow me to sign?"

"Or cross out the wagers entirely." The set of Cedric's jaw revealed his irritation.

Perry went to his library.

Cedric glowered at Alfred. "Which will it be, Alfred? All or nothing? Did you not instigate the idea?"

"N-no. I do not believe it w-was my doing."

Corey had kept her eyes away from Matthew. She did not wish to see his reaction to her demands. She knew he was part of the caper, but seeing the guilt—or the laughter—on his face might break her resolve.

When Perry brought the book into the room, Cedric took it and opened it on a delicate gilded table, flipping the pages to near the end. Perry set the ink and quill beside the book and Cedric dipped the pen. With a flourish, he drew black marks through several lines of writing.

Corey edged closer, looking for herself. Unless Cedric's blots changed the pages, it looked very much like Lord Matthew put a large amount of money on her success in fending off Cedric's efforts.

But did the book really say he wagered five hundred pounds on her success? The amount made her head spin. No wonder he had been so attentive, so careful to lurk around the corner whenever Cedric came near her.

Five hundred pounds? How absurd! Why, that was more than enough to set up her parents in Bath for several years!

She slammed the book shut. "I am disappointed your sporting impulses were not engaged by my challenge, gentlemen." She spoke the last word in her most ironic voice.

Their silence gave her a jolt of confidence. They, all four of the Quartet, were flummoxed, at least for the moment. She dipped a half-curtsy to them, whirled, and marched out of the room.

Nine

Corey sat at the little table in her bedchamber and pushed the food around on her plate. She had little appetite. When she left the drawing room with the four faces staring at her in dismay, she felt an air of triumph. But her satisfaction had not lasted long.

By the time she came up the staircase, disillusionment set in. What had she accomplished? She had shocked all of them, caused discomfiture for Cedric. Perhaps embarrassment for each of the four. She hoped they felt ashamed of their wager.

On the other hand, she lumped all four together as equal partners in their wicked escapade. Just when she had achieved real understanding and closeness with Lord Matthew, in the wake of his emotional disclosures, she had placed him right back in the category of corkbrained scoundrel playing a ludicrous, even cruel, hoax on her. A plague on that chuckleheaded Cedric for concocting such an odious wager!

She picked up her wine goblet, walked to the window, raised the sash, and leaned on the edge. From a long way off, she heard the rumble of laughter. Was it from the Quorn Quartet over dinner or from the service wing? She took a sip of the wine and thought about Lord Matthew's awful ordeal.

He admitted he had been quite unprepared for the

horrors of battle. Until he went to Belgium, he probably had never been tested by serious responsibilities. He had chafed under the protection of his father from all but the least onerous army duties. How that must have rankled him.

So in a moment of impetuous devotion to Britain's cause, he escaped his father's control and answered Wellington's call to rebuild his army. His experience changed him, drastically. Then why had he come back to join up again in the athletic exploits and preposterous antics of the Quorn Quartet?

Was he attempting to obliterate his suffering? Or trying to prove his transformation made no difference to his essential nature? Or demonstrating his strength to overcome the injury that had blown apart the muscles and nerves of his thigh?

Corey drank the last of the wine. Lord Matthew was trying to do all these things. And perhaps more. Who could blame him for wishing to wipe out the horror of the battle, the devastation of his shattered leg? What man would not wish to recapture his untroubled youth, his high spirits, however slapdash or reckless?

Corey could not blame him for trying to blot out a part of his past. In fact, it seemed quite rational. Yet it was hard to forgive him for participating in a wager aimed to compromise her. Since he had so often stepped in when Cedric pressed his attentions on her, Lord Matthew had obviously protected his outrageous bet against Cedric.

It was over now. She would have to forget any silly pretensions she might have held. Lord Matthew had not the slightest regard for her, except as the means to win a wager. There would be no more encounters in the rose garden or at the duck pond. No more fishing lessons at the stream. No more moonlit evenings on the terrace. No more gallant liberations from Cedric.

It was lucky, she mused, that she had never let herself fall in love with Lord Matthew. Oh, yes, she had spent years thinking of him, reliving that one evening in London when he stood beside her on a balcony and pressed his lips to her forehead. True, the thought of his broad shoulders and charming smile had haunted her thoughts for ages. No other man ever measured up to Matt's assortment of appealing qualities. But how fortunate that she always knew of his proclivity for reckless behavior.

Of course she had not fallen in love with him. Not in the slightest.

It would be easy to avoid all but the most offhand meetings. If they stumbled upon each other in the upcoming days, she would simply give him a nod and expect nothing in return.

"I could strangle that woman." Elaine moaned and pressed a lavender-scented hankie to her temple. Two maids stood ready to help her into a morning gown of Chinese blue.

Corey sat on a dainty slipper chair in her cousin's boudoir and tried to think of some way to alleviate Elaine's misery. "Will she not be eager to see Lord Henry and Lady Georgina?"

As soon as the words were out of Corey's mouth, a fresh torrent of moans came from Elaine. "The children dread her arrival as much as I do. They have twice as many tantrums as usual when she visits. Oh, the devil! I forgot about Lawrence! Oh, how could I?"

Corey feared Elaine would break into real tears. If

she did, her eyes would remain puffy and her nose red, giving the dowager no doubt as to the feelings of her daughter-in-law. "Elaine, stop that silly crying immediately!"

Elaine looked up in surprise. "What?"

"You cannot let the dowager see you all in tatters with traces of tears in your eyes. That is probably what she is hoping for! Buck up and meet her with a serene smile."

"But she disapproves of everything I do."

"You must not let her see it rankles. You are in charge of Lodesham Hall now, not her. Let her see that her criticism makes no impression on you."

"If only Perry did not care what she thinks . . ." Elaine's voice trailed off and she reapplied the hankie to her forehead.

At least she had not dissolved in tears, Corey noted. "Perry adores you. He only tries to appease his mama's wishes because she is, well, his mother. You would not wish him to shun her."

"Oh, you think not?"

"Elaine, just imagine what an awful example that would be to Henry and the other children. There is the future to be considered, my dear."

Elaine started in surprise. "I had never thought of it that way . . ."

"I shall go now and fetch Lawrence and Mrs. Hitchens."

"Do be sure she wears a fresh gown."

Corey nodded. "Of course. And with any luck, we should be back here before the dowager arrives."

Despite the many arrangements to be made before and during the little journey to the village and back, they were almost successful. As the basket cart came toward the house from the direction of the village, the dowager's traveling coach pulled up before the portico of the mansion. The baggage wagon passed them as Corey and Mrs. Hitchens, Lawrence in her arms, climbed out and joined Elaine in time to watch Oakley fold down the steps and help the dowager down.

The Dowager Countess of Lodesham squinted at the cluster of people before her. The frown that wrinkled her forehead deepened. "I see that Peregrine did not bother to await my arrival."

Elaine curtsied and then held her head high. "He will join us soon. For luncheon."

"Off fishing, I presume." She held up her quizzing glass and stared at Henry, who tried to hide in his mother's skirts. "Come out here, lad, and let me have a look at you."

The boy gave his grandmother a glowering look but allowed her to take his arm and pull him away from his mother.

"How old are you now, Henry?"

"Four," he murmured.

"Speak up. And do not slouch."

Henry obeyed and spoke in a louder voice, though he did not smile. "I am four."

"Where is the girl?" The dowager, Corey thought, had a winning way with children. No wonder they were less than thrilled at her visit.

Gina cowered behind Elaine.

Corey stepped up and took Gina's hand, whispering to her. "Be brave, dear, and greet your grandmama." Gently, she drew the child out before the dowager.

"Good day, Grandmama," Gina said, just as they had rehearsed that morning.

Lady Lodesham was unimpressed. "Hmmmpf. And there is another brat, I believe?"

Corey patted Elaine's arm as the quizzing glass turned to the fat little babe in Mrs. Hitchens's arms.

Elaine's voice was steady, though Corey could see the tension in her stiff back. "That is Lawrence, almost a year now."

Another indifferent snort from the dowager made Corey a believer in Elaine's low opinion of the woman. Though she had a reputation as one of Society's highest sticklers, she was anything but caring, or even civil, to her family.

Up to that moment, Corey had not noticed the two females who stood behind the dowager, neither saying a word but taking in every aspect of the scene. Because she wore a wide-brimmed bonnet, the face of the younger one was partially shaded from Corey's view. Corey supposed this was Perry's sister, Lady Sophronia. The other woman, whose grim visage surpassed even the dowager's in dour disapproval, must be the companion, as Elaine called her, the Iniquitous Ingrey.

Elaine gestured to Corey. "Mama, I hope you remember my cousin, Cordelia Bransford, who is spending the summer with us."

"I don't." The dowager turned her eyeglass on Corey. "Is she of any use to you?"

"Why, she is my guest. Though she is very good with the children."

"Too many of them, I say," the dowager muttered. "Why are we standing outside?"

Oakley quickly took Lady Lodesham's arm and helped her up the steps, where two footmen held open the doors. The daughter and companion followed, leaving Corey, Elaine, Mrs. Hitchens, and the children behind.

Corey leaned close and whispered to Elaine. "You did not exaggerate. She is a dragon, all right."

Elaine whispered back. "Wait until the Iniquitous Ingrey gets going!"

"Let's call it quits," Perry said with a growl.

Matt reeled in his line and carefully stepped out of the stream, shaking the water from his well-oiled canvas waders. "Time for the trout's midday nap, I expect."

Perry took out the book and totaled up the morning's catch. "You had a dozen, I only six."

"Losing your touch, old bean?"

Perry's shoulders were slumped, his demeanor gloomy. "At least for today. The thought of Mama's visit has Elaine in a pucker, and I do not foresee any great pleasure in it. I suspect the dowager has a purpose other than a grandparental inspection of her heirs. She don't care for children. Never did. Guess I never saw her more than half an hour a day and that was spent mostly standing at attention. Don't know how Sophronia has put up with it."

"Could have used a dose of that routine when I was nursing my leg. I had a fussing female at my side every moment, either Mama or my brother's wife. Never gave a man a moment to think."

They propped their long rods over their shoulders and began the walk to Lodesham Hall.

Perry put a period to the conversation. "Mama don't like to be predictable. She'll set things on their ear around here, mark my words."

Within the hour, refreshed and changed, Matt

thought he was prepared to meet almost any challenge. But when he heard a sharp voice from the drawing room, he almost turned around and went back to his bedchamber.

"I insist that you hold the archery competition tomorrow. I cannot stay above a week and it is perhaps the one thing you scatterbrains do that I enjoy."

As Matt entered, Perry objected, but feebly. "But, Mama, this week will be the best fishing of the entire year."

"Those trout will be there until Kingdom Come. There have always been trout in that river and you will just have to figure out a better way to extract them. If I do say so myself, you show little aptitude—"

Matt bowed to Lady Lodesham, causing her to break off her remark and give him a glimmer of a grin. "Why, Lord Matthew, it has been far too long."

He took her hand and kissed the air above it in his most cavalier style.

She gave a little wiggle of pleasure. "You always have been a flirtatious wretch, Matthew. Did I not hear you had a grave injury in the glorious defeat of that Corsican upstart?"

"A mere scratch, milady."

She surveyed him up and down with her quizzing glass. "Good thing, then, as it would have been a pity to spoil such a specimen as you."

The arrival of Alfred allowed Matt to back out of the dowager's view, noting as he did the grim-faced companion in the corner. He recalled the woman from his previous visits to the Hall, when her beady eyes and network of informants had kept Lady Lodesham informed of every move her son's friends made.

Well, almost every move. In the early years, they had delighted in schemes to misinform her.

He approached Lady Sophronia and repeated his bow. "I am pleased to see you again."

"Likewise." She dipped a curtsy and favored him with a shy smile.

Matt thought it a great pity that she resembled her mother more than her brother. Perry was reputed to look almost exactly like his father had, ruddy, blond, and handsome in a classic English way. Sophronia and her mother had sallow complexions and hair of an indeterminate shade, neither golden nor brown. "You have been enjoying the Season in London, I presume."

"Yes."

"I understand the duke has been in town."

"So I heard."

"But you did not encounter him?"

"Wellington? No."

Matt was about to try another tack when her face brightened. Alfred joined them and gave Lady Sophronia a wide smile.

"My Lady Sophronia, it is a great p-pleasure to see you." Alfred lifted her hand to his lips.

Sophronia's smile lit up her face. "I am gratified to see you, Mr. Collingwood. I have been reading the volumes by Cicero that you wrote to me about. I agree wholeheartedly with your opinions."

Matt chuckled inwardly and moved away, leaving them to converse. Unless he entirely misread the situation, Lady Sophronia and his friend Alfred were already well acquainted. Perry had once remarked that his sister was something of a bluestocking. And when he took a look back at Alfred, Matt noted with amusement the fellow was decked out like a fop, with a new waistcoat he would not have dared to wear with just the Quartet. Perhaps Lady Sophronia had a partiality for saffron stripes.

Matt took up a position near the far fireplace and surveyed the room. Perry greeted Elaine with a kiss on her cheek. Miss Bransford dipped a curtsy to the dowager and stood unspeaking while the two Ladies Lodesham spoke. Matt could tell that the words they exchanged were not happy words as the look on Elaine's face became increasingly sour. Corey wore a growing look of disbelief. The conversation was interrupted by the arrival of the final member of the party. Cedric effused over the dowager, confirming Matt's observation that the old girl liked nothing more than a chance to flirt with a younger man. Unless it was to command her son to indulge her whims.

Cedric's outrageous comments were uttered in a voice loud enough to penetrate the entire room. "Lady Lodesham, you look lovelier and younger every time I see you. I would never guess . . ."

Cedric's effusive patter gave Elaine and Corey the chance to slip away and perch on a pair of gilt chairs near the window. He walked over to stand beside them, but Miss Bransford looked away.

Elaine spoke in a voice so soft he had to lean down to catch it. "Have you ever seen a more perfect dragon, a more obnoxious old hag, Lord Matthew?"

"She seems a difficult—"

"Difficult," she hissed. "If only it were so simple."

He hoped his nod and smile released him from further comment. Corey continued to stare at the wall, quite pointedly ignoring him. He had hoped he would have the opportunity to speak with her alone for a few moments before luncheon was announced.

He was horrified at how he had dumped his problems on her after their visit to the toyshop, at what he had said about the battle. He had not meant to say so much. But he could not undo what he had already done.

Yesterday, when they had been alone, he enjoyed the fishing lesson far too much to spoil it by apologizing for the excessive way he had described the combat, for so clearly distressing her.

Then, last night, when she had so dramatically announced her knowledge of that devilish wager . . .

Of course, he could not deny his participation, no matter how much he had disapproved at its inception. Nor would she care how deeply he regretted it now. Why had he not nipped it in the bud, put an end to any such foolishness before it got started? He needed to apologize to Corey, to let her know he was truly repentant.

He hoped that Elaine might read his mind and give up her chair, but clearly she wanted to stay right where she was, well away from the dowager.

Matt tried to speak to Corey with his eyes, with his contrite smile. But she would not look his way for even an instant. Her eyes remained locked on a blank wall.

After luncheon, when the dowager demanded the presence of Elaine and the other ladies in the morning room, Elaine clutched Corey's arm and whispered. "You must not desert me, cousin."

But Corey shook her head. "But I must go see that Mrs. Hitchens gets home."

"No, no. She walked back with Lawrence more than an hour ago."

"Carrying the baby? Elaine, he is very heavy, and it is a long walk."

"Believe me, she is used to it."

The dowager broke off a list of instructions to Ingrey. "What are you two whispering about? I will not have secrets!"

"Nothing at all, simply nothing."

The men had absented themselves, with the excuse they needed the afternoon to prepare for tomorrow if they were truly to hold the archery tournament then. Corey could see they were practically praying for a storm.

In the morning room, the dowager sat on a tall chair as though it were a throne. "Miss Bransford, what is your connection to Elaine?"

"My mother and hers are sisters."

"So Lady Aylmer is your grandmother?

"Yes."

"I am surprised to see you have put your cousin in my usual bedchamber, Elaine."

Corey had urged Elaine to move her so that the dowager could have her regular place, but Elaine had refused.

Elaine mustered her courage. "You would not wish me to be unaccommodating to my own family, I am sure. It seemed unnecessary to ask her to move for the brief duration of your visit. You will be here only a week and she is staying much longer."

Corey wished she could think of some retort to give Lady Lodesham a taste of her own medicine, but she could think of nothing.

"Well, I dislike the gold room. It has too much early light."

"Then I shall have a dark drapery hung over the window for you."

"That will not be necessary. But in the future, I hope you will remember what my position is in this household."

"I had not the slightest inkling you would be coming to the Hall. I assumed you and Sophronia would be busy in London for another few weeks."

"This Season has been a great disappointment to me. And to Sophy. More than the usual number of mushrooms at every ball. And in the streets, one is constantly confronted with limbless men in ragged red coats, looking as though they expected a handout. Quite distressing to one of a gentle nature like mine."

Corey almost choked and pressed her hand to her mouth to cut off the expression of distaste that bubbled up.

"Not even Almack's had a decent supply of eligible gentlemen. Sally Jersey claims they all have gone to Paris or Rome."

"I would not doubt it," Elaine replied.

"Only Lord Rawlins paid his frequent respects to Sophronia. But she says she ain't having him."

Corey looked at Sophronia, who said nothing but gave a tiny shake of her head. Corey began to feel a little sympathy for the young lady, saddled as she was with such a mother and also the unwelcome attentions of some would-be suitor.

Lady Lodesham did not call upon Sophronia to offer her opinion nor did she turn her head to note her daughter's expression.

"In any case, when Ingrey reported that Perry was hosting his old friends in the Quorn Quartet, I thought we would come down here and see if one of them met Sophy's fancy."

Elaine looked horrified. "But Mama, you cannot expect that—"

"I can expect anything I wish. Sophy has an ample dowry and she is not getting any younger. I think it is high time she found a man with the proper breeding and sufficient resources to make her a good match. Is that not reasonable?"

Elaine looked from Corey to Sophronia and back to the dowager. "But how can you—"

"Leave it all to me. I think Lord Matthew is by far the best prospect. Do you agree?"

Corey felt like someone had dropped an anvil on her head. Lord Matthew and Lady Sophronia? It was not an impossible match, by any means. She stole a glance at Sophy, who seemed to be wiping a tear from her cheek.

Corey's own eyes burned with tears. If ever there had been a death knell for her dreams of Lord Matthew, this was it.

Ten

Corey came to dinner only because Elaine was depending upon her. Otherwise, she would have gladly forgone a single morsel of food to excuse herself from the ordeal of a formal meal with the current inhabitants of Lodesham Hall. When she came downstairs, she was surprised to find none of the men present.

Elaine's hands were clenched into white-knuckled fists, and her voice was barely audible. "If I had a dagger, I would have stabbed Perry in the heart when he told me the four of them were promised elsewhere tonight. Promised, my foot! The cowards!"

Corey did not reply, since the dowager approached with Sophronia in tow a few steps behind her. Lady Lodesham held up her quizzing glass and again surveyed Corey from head to toe.

"Pretty figure, good carriage. Hair acceptable. Amiable face."

Corey had no idea what the purpose of the survey was, but she did not much care for it. "My lady, I am not a specimen in a jar. Why are you looking at me that way?"

The dowager's cackle of laughter sounded like a broken-winged crow. "Caw! Caw! Spirit, too. I like that in a gel."

Corey found the explanation insufficient but no

more was said for all heads turned to Oakley, who announced dinner. Now, Corey thought, all she had to do was get through the meal without offending the dowager or letting open warfare break out between Elaine and the old harridan.

The dining room was bright with extra candles set in six tall, multi-branched candelabra, causing Corey to blink at the intensity of the lights. The table remained at full length and the four of them were spaced far apart, barely within shouting distance, or so it seemed to Corey.

The dowager kept up a steady monologue for the first quarter-hour. Corey paid little attention, shutting out the piercing tones of Lady Lodesham's voice as much as she could. Corey assumed Elaine and Sophy were doing precisely the same, since their faces looked as vacant as hers probably did. The only responses Lady Lodesham received were occasional mumbles. She had no trouble maintaining her monologue, however, and did not appear to be concerned with the lack of reaction.

When the dowager launched into a critique of the Hall's French chef, however, Elaine bristled. "Mama, you know Perry has very high standards when it comes to cuisine. Only the finest will do for him."

"That fellow in your kitchen hardly lets you know what you are eating. Everything is drowned in pap. I cannot distinguish the cutlets from the asparagus without scraping away the layer of cream sauce."

Elaine's voice snapped with barely suppressed anger. "It would be precisely to Lord Lodesham's taste."

"I should send him my new man to set an example.

He knows the difference between good food and covering up poor quality."

"I hope you are not inferring this food is less than the best from our own carefully nurtured supply."

"How could one tell what the food is like? It swims in cream. Perhaps I should have a word—"

Elaine looked ready to soar out of her chair. "Monsieur Jean-Paul has a delicate sensibility. I beg you not to interfere. If you drive him away, Perry will be miserable."

"Hmmpf! That boy knew what decent food was when I presided in this establishment. I fear you are far too easily influenced by a foreigner, Elaine."

Corey, who had been following the exchange with fascination, suddenly jumped into the conversation. She had almost forgotten her purpose to keep the two Ladies Lodesham from each other's throats. "You promised to tell us all about the wedding of Princess Charlotte, my lady."

After one last malicious look at her daughter-in-law, the dowager put down her fork. "The processions were magnificent, as only Prinny can concoct them . . ."

Corey cared not a fig for any of the details. She was only relieved the imbroglio over the chef ended. The chef did seem to place a dab of sauce on every dish, but she could not recall anything fully immersed. She stole a look at Elaine, who still appeared to be fuming.

". . . streets full of cheering souls . . ."

Corey wondered if Sophronia ever spoke. The young lady seemed thoroughly cowed by her mama, not that it was any surprise. It was a wonder that Perry came out of her household with such an amiable disposition. His mother's overbearing character might well explain his devotion to his friends in the Quorn Quartet.

When at last the dowager wound up her soliloquy with comments on the suitability of Oatlands for the royal wedding trip—Corey did not note if Lady Lodesham approved or disapproved—Elaine almost leaped to her feet, suggesting they call for the tea tray to be sent to the drawing room as soon as possible.

In the Ivory Saloon, the dowager stalked around the room once, as if measuring the placement of the furniture to see what might have been moved an inch or two since her reign over the house. She motioned to Ingrey. "Bring me my needlework. And Lady Sophronia's as well." She turned to Corey. "Do you stitch, missy?"

Corey's heart plunged. So far the dowager had not mentioned Elaine's condition. But if she saw Corey's little cap for the baby . . .

Ingrey spoke from the far side of the room. "I will bring Miss Bransford's work from her bedchamber. I believe she is sewing a baby's layette."

Corey swallowed her objections to having Ingrey poke around in her things. It was too late, anyway, as the woman had already marched out.

Elaine looked angry enough to chew nails.

But the dowager either had not noticed or was not ready to discuss the matter, for she jabbered on about the princess and her mother for another five minutes until Ingrey returned. When the companion handed the baby cap to the dowager, Corey almost cringed.

Lady Lodesham held the tiny white cap close to the oil lamp, inspecting both the inside and out, holding it close to her eyes, her lips tightly pursed. She took up her quizzing glass and inspected every inch of tiny stitching. At long last, she handed it back to Ingrey and stared at Corey. "Your workmanship is excellent, Cordelia."

Corey let out her breath in a sudden whoosh. Ingrey handed the cap to her and Corey looked at it as though she had never seen it before.

The dowager, as usual, had more to say. "I admire the regularity of your tiny stitches. The tucking is well done. Ingrey, show it to Sophronia."

Corey allowed Ingrey to take it and hand it to Sophy, who wore a look of painful, timid unease.

The dowager plunged on. "Sit up straight, Sophy, and look at how carefully each stitch is set."

Corey wanted nothing more than to escape this group of sorry individuals. The dowager was rude and unfeeling, Sophy miserable, and Elaine irate. What a charming tableau. But there would be no escape. For Elaine's sake, Corey would endure it to the bitter end.

The dowager took up her tapestry and commenced to jab the needle into it as vigorously as she wagged her tongue. Corey lost track of the topic.

Sophy held her canvas in one hand and stared at it with distaste. Even from several feet away, Corey could see it was poorly done. Probably under duress, never the circumstance for a first-rate effort.

Elaine had folded her hands as if to prevent them from tossing a bibelot at the dowager's head. Her facial expression would have curdled fresh milk.

Oblivious to all around her, the dowager got to the point, or at least what Corey assumed her object was.

Lady Lodesham set her needle aside. "Even though those despicable fellows abandoned us this evening, I propose, Elaine, that you speak with Lord Matthew tomorrow about the commencement of his attentions to Sophronia."

Elaine shook her head and shrugged. "Mama, Lord Matthew is all of six-and-twenty. He may—"

"Exactly! The ideal time for him to be setting up his nursery."

"But I have no influence—"

"If you think I have not been made aware of your condition, Elaine, you are mistaken. I have made my position on having so many children clear to you over the years, but you have ignored my counsel. I do not know if the gentlemen are yet aware of the situation, but I will say to you that unmarried men, in my experience, are often swayed by the fruitfulness of their friends' marriages. Men seem to find fertility a much more gratifying quality than I do."

Elaine appeared to be wordless.

The dowager hardly paused. "My plan is to conduct a little archery lesson tomorrow for Sophronia, and not to be too obvious, perhaps Cordelia as well. We will start immediately after the men conclude their competition. We will pair Lord Matthew with Sophy, then place them side by side at dinner. You, Elaine, must inform him, in a careful way, not to make him think this is preordained but largely his own idea, that Sophy has a handsome portion to bring to the match, and properties from my side of the family that will settle on her children."

Corey wished she could sink into the upholstery or evaporate into the air. She peeked over at Sophy and was surprised to see the girl's downcast face. She looked as though she might break into sobs at any moment.

The dowager's voice snapped Corey's attention back

to the subject of poor Matthew's entrapment. "As for you, Cordelia, you have no means of supporting yourself and your home in Yorkshire is a backwater of no import. I do not know what your mother has been thinking of—"

Corey wished she had the nerve to say what she thought. "I am devoted to my parents."

"That does not signify. They should be concerned with your future, not you with theirs. Since you have no help from your family, I will take over your marriage arrangements. As far as I can tell, either Mr. Williamson or Mr. Collingwood will do for you. Cedric's prospects are good from his aunt, but he is not reputed to be clever with his resources. Alfred spends far too much time poking around in old ruins, but he has a steady income. I suggest you fix upon him as your salvation. I will do my best to facilitate the match, beginning tomorrow with those lessons."

Out of the corner of her eye, Corey thought she saw Sophy wipe a tear from her cheek. *If anyone is to bawl,* Corey thought, *it ought to be me.*

The tea tray finally interrupted the dowager's harangue. Her head spinning, Corey drank quickly and, cap tucked under her arm, curtsied to the dowager. "I think I had best help Elaine upstairs, my lady."

"She looks a bit hagged. Lord knows, it is not easy having a houseful of men."

Corey practically shoved Elaine out the door before one of them lost their temper and named the real source of the household's agitation.

Once in Elaine's boudoir, both of them dropped onto chairs as if they carried loads of solid stone on their shoulders.

Corey closed her eyes and sighed. "I never imagined your descriptions of the dowager would be mild in comparison with the way she has behaved today."

"From one visit to the next, even I forget how truly dreadful she is."

"Did she ask you about my parents?"

"Oh, no, Corey. Ingrey tells her all of it. The woman wrings information out of the servants and probably keeps notes on every family in the realm. You can be sure that she knew all there was to know about Matthew, Cedric, and Alfred before she left London. I am sure that she read every letter from your parents you left in your room. She is a viper!"

"My very own letters?"

"Oh yes, you can be sure of it. And you are in the suds now. You might as well start stitching on your trousseau for your wedding to Alfred Collingwood!"

Corey groaned. She did not intend to marry. Her real concern now was the dowager's companion, though she would never admit it to Elaine.

All day, Corey had been surreptitiously watching Ingrey. If Corey became a companion, would she be expected to collect information, to spy on others and provide that intelligence to her employer? Would she be as unwelcome in houses where her employer was a guest?

Corey knew very little of the London penchant for gossip. She remembered the encyclopedic knowledge that some society ladies boasted, as though they had memorized the pages of one of those guides to the aristocracy. She hoped the lady who eventually hired her as companion would look for more agreeable traits, such as a nice reading voice, a facility with needlework, and a strong arm to lean on when walking in the garden. She could also suggest her ability to arrange flowers and work in the stillroom. But these seemed meager attributes and qualifications.

She thought again about Ingrey and how the woman's dark little eyes darted around the room. Corey could hardly prevent a little shudder. When she became a companion, she would no longer be a guest like she was here at Lodesham Hall. Companions were relegated to servants' quarters. They might expect to take tea with the housekeeper or a governess, but not with the household guests. Companions sat alone in a corner of a room, prepared to jump up and fetch or carry for a crotchety old lady. Or listen to every conversation and report its content.

Corey looked over at Elaine's closed eyes. "Cousin, dear, I shall call Sawyer for you and head for bed myself. It has been a . . . a . . . I cannot think how to characterize this day."

"Nor can I, Corey. Nor can I."

The next morning, Matt paused in the corridor outside the breakfast room. The dowager was still there, and announced her intention of going directly to the field set aside for the archery contest.

"It is a good thing I am here today, for I am sure you would not remember all the precautions necessary to make this competition safe and fair, Perry. I have arranged for the staff to assist me."

Matt tried to slip into a chair without being noticed, but Lady Lodesham shook her finger at him.

"Good morning, you darling boy. I hope you realize I will be presiding this afternoon, Matthew. You know how I always made sure you boys played fair!"

"Yes, my lady, you did indeed."

Cedric sat across the table, rolling his eyes.

The dowager looked around with her nearsighted squint. "I have forbidden Perry from doing any boxing. I find it vulgar in the extreme and I will not allow it!"

After breakfast, to bolster Perry's flagging morale, Matt accompanied him toward the archery field, along with Cedric and Alfred. They stopped a good ways away, shielded from the dowager's view by the wall of the kitchen garden.

"Don't trip on the beans or stomp on a cucumber seedling," Perry warned them. "Mama would hear of it within moments and our penalties would be severe."

Cedric nodded. "She has an amazing set of informants. Rivals anything Wellington had against the frogs."

"I need not point out, I am sure, why Elaine has retired to her bed for the day."

"Tempted to do so myself," Cedric said.

Perry placed his elbow atop the wall and propped his chin on his palm. "When Mama arrives, I always feel I am about ten years old again. She rearranges everyone's life. Especially Elaine's. Not to mention you fellows. And poor Miss Bransford, according to my wife, has also caught the tartness of Mama's tongue."

Alfred looked thoughtful. "I am surprised your sister seems so even-tempered."

"Sophronia has little choice. Mama will have it no other way. Sophy has learned to be complacent and compliant. She will make some man an excellent wife, if she maintains that biddable demeanor."

Matt watched two men walking out the distance to the targets. To his eye, it looked accurate. "Does she know much about archery competitions? I would have thought that a rather arcane subject for a lady of fashion."

"Mama knows all there is to know about every topic of interest to anyone within her acquaintance. She makes it her purpose to know these things. She is as unerring in her acquisition of facts as she is of gossip and matters of morality. One defies her with the greatest of caution. I can only say I am surprised she has shown up here. For the last several years she has visited only at Christmas and we went to her for a very brief stay at Easter."

The men in the field had set up three targets and were now engaged in painting lines on the grass to mark the three distances from which they would shoot at the targets.

The dowager's chair sat beneath a sunshade from which she directed the servants, apparently having recruited the butler Oakley to convey her wishes to the others. The comfort of the observers as well as the competitors was assured by a wagonload of provisions set up on tables as though it were a gathering of the *ton*.

As they watched, the basket cart came into view, pulled by a fat, plodding pony. It was an awkward equipage, but practical. "Where did you find that pony cart, Perry?"

Alfred chuckled as though seeing it for the first time. "Cumbersome th-thing."

"I had it made—that is, I had the willows woven to build up the sides. I did not want the children falling out."

Matt was impressed. "Very clever, I'd say."

"I suppose we ought to move on over there soon. I feel like a calf to the slaughter."

Matt watched Miss Bransford follow Henry out of the basket cart. She took his hand and walked toward the dowager. What could Lady Lodesham possibly have found to criticize about Cordelia?

Despite the onerous burden of adhering to every one of the dowager's many strictures, Matt enjoyed the archery competition. She insisted that they sit down for refreshments between each of the three rounds, which gave his aching leg several excellent rests. Before they began the final round, he spoke to Henry.

"Are you anxious to find yourself a little bow and give this sport a try, young man?"

"Oh yes, I will ask Papa to find me a bow just the right size. I went with him to Dorchester when he bought the new arrows, you know."

The scores were almost even when the four men took their places at the line most distant from the target. It was Perry's turn to shoot first, and he took great care to aim, draw the bow, and re-aim. The arrow flew straight to the target and, with a thump, penetrated its canvas cover, but well without the inner ring. Perry muttered an imprecation and shot again, this time only slightly missing the bull's eye. Alfred stepped up to the line and let fly two arrows in rapid succession, both coming very near the center. The dowager and Sophronia applauded, and Alfred favored them with a bow.

"Get over here, you ridiculous ham," Cedric said.

The dowager called on Oakley to note the score of each shot, then marked down the score. "Who is shooting now?" she asked after each arrow.

Matt suspected she could not see far enough to tell the shooters apart. Why she had not acquired spectacles, he could not imagine.

Cedric waved to the audience and drew his bow. Just as he was about to let the arrow fly, the pony gave a sudden neigh. Cedric's arrow barely nicked the edge of the target.

Matt almost laughed out loud. "I say, bad luck!"

"Blasted nag," Cedric moaned. "Can I take it over or will you hold me to my shot?"

"Does that count?" Perry called to the dowager.

She nodded majestically. "Why not? No knight in the field would have been shooting in silence."

"Curses." Cedric took another arrow and sent it straight to the very center of the bull's eye.

But his missed shot had been enough to tip the score and send Perry's effort to the top of the scorecard by a mere two points over Matt and three over Alfred.

Corey could tell the conclusion of the archery tournament put the dowager in a festive mood. Lady Lodesham obviously approved of the scores favoring her son and Lord Matthew, the man she had chosen for her daughter.

But Sophronia seemed less interested in Lord Matthew than in braiding, untangling, and rebraiding the fringe on her shawl. Instead of following her mother's instructions and putting herself forward to Lord Matthew, Sophy sat quietly staring into the distance when she was not fiddling with her fringe. To Corey, Sophy's behavior seemed beyond explanation. She seemed completely uninterested in Lord Matthew Allerton, no matter what her mother had in mind for them. Perhaps she thought of Matt only as the mischievous cohort of her older brother. She probably knew nothing of Matthew's war injury, of his bravery, nothing of the depth of character he buried under the polished facade of the Corinthian. Sophy must still think him as roguish and ill-behaved as the other members of the Quorn Quartet.

Like Corey, Sophronia had grown up as a younger sister of a playful and coddled elder brother, who had dominated the concerns of their parents. Sophy, like Corey, may have meant little to her parents except as a potential alliance with another prominent family. Sophy's shyness was not so surprising when one considered how she probably developed her own quiet interests in the face of her mama's overwhelming need to dominate everyone and everything.

When the celebratory wineglasses were empty, the dowager directed the servants to gather the bows and prepare for the lessons. Corey wanted nothing more than to go back to the house and check on Elaine, but she felt sure the dowager would demand she fulfill those orders to participate in the archery instruction.

Alfred picked up a quiver of arrows. "I suggest you leave your bonnets here, ladies. The brims will only impede your aim."

Lord Matthew helped Sophy and Alfred assisted Corey to lace on protective leather gloves. Then, carrying two bows and a handful of arrows, they escorted them to the center of the field to the shooting line closest to the target. Corey was surprised to note the eagerness with which Sophy joined in. Perhaps she was not so lifeless as Corey had imagined. Sophy now had a smile on her face and her eyes were bright with anticipation.

Alfred stood next to Corey in the position closest to the sidelines. He instructed her to hold the bow correctly. She was surprised at the strength it took to draw the bow, and she flexed her shoulders several times to rid them of tension. When she looked at Alfred for his assessment of her progress, he was not looking at her at all; rather, he was watching Lady Sophronia, who appeared to stare at him in return. Lord Matthew kept his distance.

Alfred stepped close to Sophronia. "Here, my lady, let me help you." He wrapped his arms around her, placing his hands on hers and pulling back on the string a few times. She gazed up at him with a look that spoke volumes.

Corey realized the truth of the situation now. The only times Sophy seemed animated were when she spoke with Alfred. Corey looked over at the dowager, just far enough away that with her weak eyesight she might not be able to distinguish Alfred from Lord Matthew. Both, after all, wore buff-colored breeches and coats of dark blue. Corey spread her arms wide, trying to block as much of the view as possible and pulled the bow back several more times.

"May I assist you?" Lord Matthew took the same position with Corey that Alfred had with Sophy. Matt's chest pressed against Corey's back and his arms lifted hers, just as they had when he was teaching her to cast the fishing line.

She wished she could wiggle away and insist on Alfred's help. But where would that leave Sophy?

Corey had enjoyed the sensations of her nearness to Matt a few days ago. Now she wanted only to express her anger at him, stomp on his boots, or elbow him in the ribs. But his hands were warm on hers, and his fingers helped her stretch the bow twice as far as she managed alone. She wished she could expunge the shivery sensations that played across her back.

"Miss Bransford," Matt whispered, "have you ever shot an arrow?"

"I would think my lack of experience was quite obvious, Lord Matthew. I can hardly pull the drawstring at all."

"Then perhaps we should practice this way every morning, noon, and evening. I am sure that in a few weeks, your arms will develop stronger muscles."

There was something too provocative in his low tones and teasing timbre. "I thought you were supposed to be teaching Sophronia. Alfred was to be my instructor."

"Do you find the change in position objectionable?"

"I assume the dowager Lady Lodesham finds it so."

"We are conspiring to ensure that she does not realize what is happening. Cedric is diverting her with the full magnitude of his charm, and Perry will do his best to call her attention away from us in case Cedric's efforts falter."

For another quarter-hour, they kept up the pretense of the archery lessons, even sending a few arrows toward the targets, though all fell far short. In spite of her continuing antagonism toward Matt, Corey found a little satisfaction at the thought of deluding the dowager so completely.

By the time they were finished with all the arrows, Corey felt quite flushed, partially with the exertion of the archery and partially with the way in which Lord Matthew's arms embraced her. "I am afraid I have crushed your neck cloth, Lord Matthew."

He gave a low, rumbly laugh and his breath tickled

her ear. "I assure you, my dear, I am not concerned with my cravat. I assume that when the dowager gets a close look at me, she will find those creases most satisfactory, as she will assume her daughter put them there."

"I hope you realize what restraint I have used, good sir. I could have used this moment to settle a few scores with you, but for the benefit of Lady Sophronia, I have curbed myself."

"Then I suggest we meet after dinner, Cordelia. For there are two sides to every quarrel!"

Eleven

Matt found the dinner impossibly tedious. The food was almost inedible, the result, Perry whispered, of an outburst of temper in the kitchen following a visit from the dowager. Perry had sent the offended Jean-Paul on a visit to Bath to take the waters for a few days.

The quality of the conversation rivaled the menu for boredom. Only when Cedric diverted her with his flirtatious teasing did the dowager Lady Lodesham stop for breath.

Matt tried to engage Cordelia's gaze, but as she had that afternoon, Miss Bransford stubbornly refused to look his way. It seemed hours passed before the ladies went to the drawing room and more hours before Perry reluctantly suggested the men join the ladies.

But it was not long thereafter before Corey murmured her excuses and slipped from the room. Matt followed her with what he hoped was a touch of discretion, and caught up with her just as she started up the staircase.

"Miss Bransford, may I have a word with you?"

She turned slowly, a frown crinkling her brow. "Just a word."

They went into the morning room where only one lamp was lit, the wick turned very low. The light was dim, but he could see her face clearly as soon as his eyes adjusted.

"I need to speak with you, Miss Bransford. I need to explain that wager. It was a terrible mistake, we have all agreed, quite over the top. I sincerely apologize."

She said nothing. Her face was expressionless.

"I hope you do not hold it against me, Miss Bransford?"

She tilted her head to one side and spoke in a voice full of derision. "Now, why would I do that? Because you wagered on the preservation of my virtue? Or was it simply a case of opposing Mr. Williamson and Mr. Collingwood, the desire to defeat your friendly opponents? I suppose it was one of those matters of sport you Corinthians revered so highly."

He could find no words to defend himself.

She was not finished. "I seem to recall you were on hand to come to my assistance several times when Cedric imposed on me. Certainly he was not prepared to use force and thus ruin his so-called honor as a Corinthian." She pronounced the final word scornfully.

"Cedric and I . . ." He did not know what to say.

"By the standards you seem to hold dear, Lord Matthew, he would not have been successful whether you had intervened or not. I was anything but susceptible to his suit. I hardly needed assistance."

Matt felt the prick of anger begin to grow. "Tell me, Miss Bransford, did you kiss him? Either in the past few days or in London a few years ago?"

Her voice was even more acidic than his. "Why, that is a very rude question. Of what concern is it to you?"

He wished he could say, *because I have wanted to kiss you.* But he did not say anything of the kind. He only smiled, one eyebrow arched.

Her face began to lose its calm. Her eyes narrowed and the frown deepened. "I will answer you. Yes, I did kiss Mr. Williamson. But it was not as a result of his insistence or my regard for him. It was pure curiosity!" She walked away, then whirled and faced him again. "What is it these young women are so enraptured about? A meeting of mouths? Why are mere kisses so heavy with significance that poets extol them and ladies faint? I found kissing Cedric quite unremarkable. Quite ordinary, no different from kissing one's papa or bussing a favorite pet. The fabled heart-stopping excitement was not evident in my experience with Mr. Williamson."

"Bravo, Miss Bransford." He stepped toward her and pulled her into his arms, then slowly passed his lips over hers, back and forth several times before slipping a hand behind her head. He tasted her, inhaled her fragrance, felt her lips soften and open beneath his as she melted against his chest with a little sigh.

What started out to be a lesson for her became a lesson for him, a lesson in emotions he never thought he would feel. The raging desire to hold her close, to make her his own. The flames that shot through his blood frightened him. This was more than he had ever intended.

With care he set her away and took a deep breath. "Now, Miss Bransford, have you been sufficiently disabused of your notion that kisses between a man and a woman are no different from getting a swipe from a pup's tongue?"

She stood wide-eyed, trembling a little, and said nothing. Either she, too, had been overcome by the depth of their passion, or she was gathering her anger for a verbal tirade.

He was reeling himself, though he summoned his usual smooth smile to cover his confusion.

In a moment she seemed to recover. "So, in canceling the wager on Mr. Williamson's ability to compromise me, Lord Matthew, did you replace it with your wager to accomplish a similar feat?"

"Shhhh!" He took her in his arms again and pressed her close.

She leaned against him and whispered. "Why are you doing this, Lord Matthew, if it is not to win a bet?"

"Shhhhh."

He kissed her again.

A loud cough rumbled through the air. He looked up to see the shocked expression of the dowager and a leering grin on Cedric's face.

"Cease at once!" The dowager's voice crackled in the air.

Corey jumped out of his arms.

Lady Lodesham's eyes glittered in the dark room. "I assume you are prepared to deal with the consequences of this behavior, Lord Matthew. Cordelia, I am shocked you would allow such a thing."

Matt wrapped his arm around Corey's shoulders. "Lady Lodesham, of course it was our intention to surprise all of you with our plans. Miss Bransford is about to make me the most fortunate of men—"

Corey's heart turned to ice. What was he saying? She found her voice, even if it was barely a croak. "No, no. There are no plans. There will be no plans."

Lord Matthew continued as though she had not opened her mouth. "We will marry as soon as—"

Corey squeezed his hand. "We most certainly will not! That is, I am not going to—"

He squeezed back until she winced. "Your interruption is most untimely, my lady. As you can see, our future is under discussion and we have—"

The dowager uttered one fateful word. "Obligation. You have both engaged an obligation to one another and I will brook no interference with the prompt announcement of your betrothal."

"But there is no betrothal . . ." Corey's words evaporated into the gathering darkness. The dowager had turned on her heel, and dragging Cedric alongside her, disappeared behind the arbor.

Lord Matthew stroked her shoulder. "Caught, Miss Bransford. We were well and truly caught."

"Nonsense. No ill-tempered old lady is going to force us to wed when we do not wish to do so. I will not be pushed into anything. I cannot imagine such a hopeless way to begin a marriage."

"I take full responsibility for compromising you. I will do my duty."

"Your duty is the same as mine, Matthew—to be true to yourself. I have no intention of tying you to a colorless chit like me. You could have a great career in the government. You need to marry a lady whose family can join with yours in helping you advance."

"Your family is part of one of the oldest in the kingdom."

"Only a very poor and distant twig, not even a branch on the family tree."

"And you are related by marriage to the very influential dowager Countess of Lodesham, her son the earl, and your cousin, his countess. I think that adds up to an impressive pedigree."

"As that dowager would say, 'Fustian!'"

"Miss Bransford, do I have some dreadful quality you despise? Is my suit so very distasteful to you?"

"Do not be a numbskull! Now unhand me!"

To her very great disappointment, he did exactly that.

As soon as she turned a corner in the corridor and was out of Lord Matthew's sight, Corey broke into a run and dashed up the stairs to her room.

Panting, she threw herself across the bed. Her breathlessness was due more to his kisses, the warmth of his arms, than to her exertions in escaping to safety.

Oh, yes, Lord Matthew. Oh, yes. There was not a trace left of the thought that kisses were mundane, ordinary. Kisses were every bit as dangerous as the novels said. Just as full of the peril generations of mothers had warned their daughters about. Just as heavenly and as intoxicating as the wordsmiths said.

She wished his kisses could have gone on forever.

Except that he was toying with her. She hoped she had not shown a fatal vulnerability. And she especially hoped he did not have another wager. Oh, how she wished he had meant those kisses, that he truly had some affection for her. How lovely that would be.

But how impossible!

As for offering to marry her, he would soon have regretted that statement if she had acceded to the dowager's demands. Corey guessed Lord Matthew had been kind to her for reasons besides winning the wager with Cedric, but such kindness would not extend to a lifelong obligation.

By tomorrow, Corey strongly suspected the dowager

would regret her words to Lord Matthew about doing his duty to Corey. Just this afternoon, Lady Lodesham had talked about marrying Lord Matthew to her daughter. Sophronia had yet to be heard on the subject, but she seemed an entirely biddable girl, unlikely to defy her mother's choice. Whether Lord Matthew would have acceded to Lady Lodesham's wishes was another matter.

If a man were to pick a wife and had to choose between Sophy and herself, Cordelia wondered how he would make the decision. Sophy had family and money on her side. Plus she seemed obedient, submissive, and docile. Corey had very little to compare to Perry's sister. Perhaps she could count a certain liveliness as an asset. Her birth was respectable if not outstanding. But she had no dowry and was unlikely to inherit a shilling. She was probably prettier than Sophy, but dressed properly, perhaps the taller Sophy would be more regal, more elegant.

Yet what was the chance that Lord Matthew would consider marrying at all? How much less troublesome for a rakish fellow like him to set up a lightskirt he could visit at his own convenience. Corey was not too green to understand that many men, both married and single, had such arrangements.

Perhaps Sophronia was amenable to a marriage of convenience, without having attracted the affections of her husband. But Corey was not interested in that kind of alliance. If Corey married, she swore it would be to a man she adored and who adored her.

Which meant she would probably never marry, for she could not deny her strong feelings for Lord Matthew, feelings which he did not return. A one-sided match was out of the question, even if she had found him willing. Better she should go away and find employment, alone with her broken dreams, than be a wife in name only.

No, anything beyond a casual flirtation did not fit his plans. She might as well start to strip thoughts of him from her brain and feelings for him from her heart. Starting now.

She wiped her eyes and blew her nose.

A tapping at the door made her sit up straight. "Come."

Elaine burst in, her hand clasped to her mouth, and flopped down on the bed. "My dear, you are a genius. You are too brilliant for words!"

Corey could not believe her ears. "What are you saying?"

Elaine sputtered with laughter. "Ingrey demanded that Perry send for the physician. I have never been so diverted in my life!"

"I do not understand what you are saying."

"Corey, the dowager has had an attack of palpitations, intense spasms that have caused her to take to her bed. But she is not really ill. She is so angry she cannot bear to speak to anyone. You and Lord Matthew played your roles brilliantly. How did you dream up such a drama?"

"The dowager did not look like she was feeling faint when she confronted us."

"Oh, it was the shock. Once she realized what she had seen and what she said, that her plans for Sophy were thwarted, she grew so red in the face, Ingrey made her lie down. Old Ingrey is herself speechless with rage."

Corey felt the world was spinning so fast her brain could not keep up with it.

Elaine bubbled on. "You and Matt must have dreamed it up while you were pretending to learn to draw a bow. I could see you two whispering out there. And so did the dowager. So when both of you disappeared after dinner, she fell right into your scheme and came looking for you."

"What did Lord Matthew have to say?"

"He has disappeared for the moment. Perry is excessively amused, but of course he has to help his mama. Sophy ran away, too."

"Poor thing. Does she wish to marry Lord Matthew? She did not look very happy about the plan last night."

"I have no idea. She says nary a word when her mother is near. One would assume she would like to escape the dowager, but perhaps the old harridan has threatened to come live with her when she marries."

Corey tried to absorb the news from downstairs, but the shadows in her head kept shifting. Obviously Elaine had jumped to a mistaken conclusion, but Corey felt no need to enlighten her at the moment.

Elaine could not stop giggling. "Oh, how I wish I had been there to see the whole thing! Cedric said you two were quite convincing. Was it your idea or Matthew's?"

"Are you sure the dowager will be all right?"

"Exaggeration comes naturally to her. I think she collapsed because she did not know how to deal with such a masterfully accomplished downfall. Tell me all the details. What did she say when she discovered you?"

Corey was not sure she could remember the exact words. "She shook her finger and told us to stop at once. Something about being ashamed of me."

"And then she demanded that Matthew marry you, or so Cedric reported."

"Of course, I refused. How ridiculous to think a kiss or two requires a man to make an offer."

Elaine abruptly stopped laughing and stared straight into Corey's eyes. "Cordelia, wait a moment. Do you mean that Lord Matthew told the dowager you had an understanding? Why, that makes an even better scam. But why did you demur? Do not tell me he was serious!"

Suddenly Corey realized how useful Elaine's interpretation would be. "Of course he was not."

"Good. For a minute there, I was afraid . . ."

"I am afraid your mother-in-law took things far more seriously than we intended."

Elaine leaned over and kissed Corey's cheek. "I want to meet with the doctor before he sees her, so I will see you in the morning, my clever, clever cousin!"

Corey sank back on her pillow after Elaine left. One could never predict the next twist things might take in this most odd of all summers.

No one had yet found him in his comfortable retreat, Matt mused, and tonight he was grateful for its refuge. He propped his leg up and stretched out along the seat of the barouche. If he hadn't been the cause of all the commotion, he was sure he would have found it most humorous. Poor Cordelia, just discovering the appeal of kisses, so rudely interrupted.

But what had caused her to be so adamant about refusing him? She was downright vociferous in her repudiation of his little fib. He had been speaking more to placate the dowager than to insist on Corey's hand. But she made no bones about it! She was resolute in her denial of his suit.

She said she would not be pushed into anything. She really was a game little lady.

The next morning Corey was grateful she had an excuse to leave the house with the children. It took little convincing of Mrs. Newsome to see they had a little lunch packed for today's picnic. After the extravaganza of yesterday on the improvised archery range, the sudden departure of Jean-Paul, and the dramatics of last night's collapse of the dowager, Corey knew the servants would be only too happy to adhere to her requests for simplicity.

Henry was full of news when he, Gina, and Bess joined Corey in the basket cart. "Grandmama has to stay in bed all day. She has spatters."

Corey kept her grin to herself. "Do you mean spasms?"

"I guess so. Mama says Grandmama is going to be fine, but she makes a lot of noise."

"Sometimes people do that when they are unwell."

In the cart, Henry picked up his sailboat and cradled it in his arms. "Will Lord Matthew come to help me sail the Zephyr today?"

Corey sincerely hoped not. She had a great many things to discuss with Lord Matthew but none of them involved boats. "I do not think so, Henry. I believe your father and the other men will be after the trout again today."

"Can we go watch them?"

"Perhaps later, closer to midday. For the moment we will sail your boat on the duck pond."

The children, perhaps not wishing to return home any more than Corey did, were remarkably happy to play while Corey sewed the dress for Gina's doll. The pony grazed greedily in the long grass and the groom dozed under the trees.

As the morning wore on, Corey wondered what Lord Matthew thought of last night. Had anyone told him that Elaine called it a superb joke, a stunt they dreamed up to annoy the dowager? Would he explain the true situation?

And what of those kisses? Again she struggled to explain her reaction. That rush of feelings she could not describe in words. That shivery, trembly sensation in her nerves, her knees, her entire being. That peculiar excitement that filled her heart and made her want to hold him closer. All of it was beyond her understanding.

She could only hope to put it out of her mind. Perhaps someday she would comprehend what happened to her when Lord Matthew began kissing her. She was very afraid it might be part of falling in love.

Henry's voice broke into her reverie. "Corey, Corey. My string is running out."

Puffs of wind had blown his boat almost all the way across the pond. She hurried to his side. "Can you tug it back?"

"It is pulling hard."

The reel of string, almost all played out, continued to unroll. The breeze had filled the distant sail and Henry could hardly keep it steady, tugging on it as hard as he could. Before she could grab it from his hand, the string snapped and the boat glided free, toward the far side of the pond.

Henry was ready to cry. "Now what do we do?"

Corey watched the little craft sail farther and farther away. Instead of lodging in the weeds at the edge of the pond, it seemed to be heading for the broad expanses of the flooded water meadows that connected eventually to the river.

"Henry, I think we need a rowboat. So we better set off for the trout streams and find your father and Lord Matthew."

By the time the basket cart was loaded with all their things, the little boat had sailed entirely out of sight.

Corey hugged Henry, who was on the verge of tears, and patted Gina's head. For once she was not teasing her brother about his loss.

They lumbered slowly toward the river. Corey imagined the beautiful sailboat disappearing in one of the thousands of clumps of weeds, or tipping over behind a fallen log. How would they ever find it? She almost wanted to cry herself.

When they neared the favored fishing spots, Corey took Gina's hand and tried to keep Henry from running and tumbling over a rock or a root as they covered the last few yards to the men. He forged ahead without minding her in the slightest, forgetting all the rules about making noise near the stream. "Papa, Papa. Lord Matthew!"

He ran too far ahead for Corey to shush him.

Lord Matthew was the closest to them. "What's wrong, Henry?" He waded out of the water and scooped the boy into his arms.

"My boat. My Zephyr. It is gone."

Perry was nearby. "Henry? Are you all right?"

In answer to the question, Henry began to snuffle. "My boat."

Corey hurried to explain the loss of the wayward vessel. "So I thought if we took a rowboat, we might find it on the water meadows."

Lord Matthew handed Henry into his father's arms.

Perry hugged his boy, but shook his head. "Talk about a needle in a haystack."

Lord Matthew took out his pocket watch. "You are due back at the house in half an hour, Perry."

"Yes, and Mama will surely suffer a relapse if I do not return on time. Perhaps we can look for the boat later in the afternoon, Henry."

The boy hid his face and wept. "No. I want to go now. My boat . . ."

Lord Matthew gathered up his gear. "I will tell you what, Henry—you and Gina go home with your father. Miss Bransford will remember where the boat was headed. She and I will hunt down the Zephyr."

Corey quickly protested. "I should go back with the children. They have not had their picnic yet—"

"All the better," Matt said. "They can have luncheon at home, and we will eat the picnic while we search."

Perry set Henry on his feet. "Sounds like the ideal solution."

"But I thought . . ." Corey could not think of any objection other than her reluctance to be alone with Lord Matthew.

He reached for her hand. "We have no time to waste. Where is the luncheon?"

Corey went to the cart and hung the hamper over her arm. Perhaps it would keep him from touching her.

Perry waved good-bye as he rode away with the children, Gina sober and quiet, Henry still teary-eyed.

Lord Matthew gave them a salute, and took the hamper from Corey's arm. "Allow me to carry this, Miss Bransford. I think our little excursion will give us an ample opportunity to settle a few things between us."

The rowboat was moored upriver near the channels that led to the lakes, the water meadows, and even the duck pond. Matt held the boat while Corey climbed in, then set the picnic hamper in front of her. He sat down and started to row. "There is a maze of waterways here. We need to keep to the deeper canals or we shall find ourselves aground, stuck on the grass. When these meadows flood every spring, the water may be only inches deep in many places."

"Is anything marked?"

"The first thing we have to find is the channel leading out of the river. There is a screen placed there to keep the fish in the river. When we find it, we have to keep the church steeple directly behind us. The channel to the lake is quite straight, and there is a cutoff that leads to the pond."

Corey was actually glad the route was complicated, for it kept them from talking about other matters. The only sound for a few moments was the singing of the birds and the splash of the oars. She kept her eye on the bank, trying to pick out the location of the channel. Along the waterline, many tiny flowers bloomed among the weeds.

She noticed what looked like a tangle of saplings in the shallows. "Could that be it?"

He turned and squinted at the bank. "I think it might be."

He edged the boat nearer and, with one of the oars, pushed at the mass of twigs, branches, and weeds caught in the network of woven saplings. When the storm's litter was cleared away and floating downstream, he unhooked the screen and opened it inward like a gate. "This is designed to keep all but the tiniest fish in the main river. If they got into the water meadows, they could be stranded when the water recedes if there is a dry spell."

"I had never thought of a gate in a river."

"A few years ago, we spent several days strengthening it. Perry has a high regard for his trout of all ages."

Sitting behind Matt and facing the back of the boat, Corey saw what he meant about keeping the steeple directly behind them. On either side of their wake, the banks became indistinct, water spilling over the grass in meandering rivulets of indistinguishable depth. The land was so flat, it seemed a calm sea of water and grass as far as the eye could see. Tufts of grass and weeds were everywhere.

She saw no sign of a little sailboat. "Do you think it could have come this far?"

"Not quite. If we can find the way into the duck pond, we'll turn around and start over."

She shaded her eyes against the glare off the water. The sailboat was tiny compared to the vast area of the flooded meadows. How would they ever find it?

Abruptly Matt slowed his strokes and let the oars rest. "Seems to me we ought to be almost at the turn for the pond."

Corey could not see a single feature of the landscape that looked familiar. "It seemed breezier when we were at the pond and it was blowing directly away from us."

"Then if we find the turn, we should be headed in the right direction to find it."

Unless, Corey worried, it was wedged into a clump of weeds, hidden from any but the closest view.

Matt pulled hard on one of the oars. "I think this is it, about here." The boat turned and almost immediately bumped to a stop.

Corey grabbed the gunnels to keep her seat.

Matt gave a bark of laughter. "Guess I miscalculated. Hold on, Cordelia."

With a mighty backward stroke he dislodged them from the shallows and the boat floated back into the main channel. "I know we are close."

It took two more attempts, one requiring him to climb out and wrench the boat out of the weeds, before they found the way toward the pond.

Matt turned around to give her a wry smile when they finally realized they were on the right course. "I seem to be a bit rusty in my navigational skills, Corey. But I think we have it now."

"Seems to me a miracle you found it at all. Everything is exactly like everything else, the same wherever I look. I would say you have earned your admiral's decorations."

He laughed out loud. "Only if we rescue the lost frigate, matey. Now, Corey, if you turn around and face the bow of this little craft, you can watch for it ahead."

Careful not to tip the boat, Corey followed his suggestion. She squinted against the shimmering light off the water and could make out nothing but tufts of grass and weeds. "I can't see a thing that looks like a sailboat."

"We have a little ways to go to the pond. I am kicking myself for having too short a string on the reel. And for not making it stronger."

"I thought it came that way from the shop."

"It did, but I should have known—"

"Wait! I see something!" Corey thought she saw movement ahead but a cloud passed over the sun and she lost it. "Go slowly. When the sun comes out again I think I will be able to see it."

He held the oars out of the water and let the boat drift, turning around and looking where Corey pointed.

The cloud moved away and in the distance, there was definitely a triangular-shaped object coming their way. Corey could see it was not a duck but it might be a branch drifting with the breeze.

Matt pulled hard on the oars, propelling the boat rapidly forward.

"Yes! I think we have it!" Corey was so pleased she almost felt like crying. "Oh, Matt, you have done it."

In just moments, they snatched the Zephyr out of the water, no worse for its unscheduled voyage.

Corey did not mind the water drops on her skirt. "We must hurry back and tell Henry!"

Matt gave her a whimsical smile. "Not until I have my reward, Cordelia. The reward that only you can give."

Her heart thumped in her chest. Would he have the nerve to kiss her right out in the sunshine in the middle of the water meadows?

He settled back at the oars. "I intend to get into that pond and find a place to pull up on the bank. Then you and I can get back on land and indulge ourselves in a little celebration."

From head to toe, she felt little tremors of anticipation, and mentally gave herself a pinch. Whatever had come over her to hope he might take her in his arms again?

"I only wish there was a bottle of wine in that hamper to go along with our cold chicken."

Corey giggled out loud.

Matt turned to look at her. "What is so funny about that?"

"Oh, nothing. Nothing at all. I was just thinking that the lemonade jar will be rather warm by the time we get to it." So much for kisses. He had been thinking only of his stomach!

Twelve

A half-hour later, Corey closed up the hamper on the remains of their luncheon. Matt had devoured three of the little iced cakes the children adored. Now, he lay on one side and idly chewed on a blade of grass.

As she watched him, her pulse beat harder again. If ever they were going to discuss last night, the time had arrived.

He tossed the blade of grass aside and lifted his gaze to hers, giving her a slow, inquiring smile. He had never looked more delicious.

She had to restrain the urge to lie down beside him, for so the invitation in his eyes seemed to request. Surely he could hear the pounding of her heartbeat.

She tore up a piece of bread and tossed it to the ducks. Their quacking usually made her smile, but not now.

She knew he was preparing to laugh off their intimacy last night. He would admit it was all a hum, designed to annoy the dowager, just as Elaine had imagined. She would shrug and laugh it away.

But inside, would she be crying? Or relieved? After a whole night and morning of sorting through the wide variety of confused feelings she had for him, she was no closer to comprehending her own mind.

He sat up and brushed off his wading boots. "Corey, why did you refuse my offer last night?"

"Was that what it was, my lord? An offer of marriage?"

"Well, perhaps not in so many words. But I was not speaking in jest. I am quite prepared to marry you."

Corey wished she had detected a glimmer of enthusiasm in his words. "It is not necessary."

"You may think differently if the dowager decides to spread your name around the drawing rooms of London."

Corey almost broke into laugher. "Lord Matthew, who would know of my name in a single London drawing room? It is your name that will be noted. And I seem to recall that the exploits of young men kissing maidens in the country is hardly a matter for censure. A day or two of gossip, perhaps, but nothing more. My reputation does not exist in London. Your reputation will be quite safe."

"You might be surprised what this story could do, Corey. Certainly it would be an embarrassment to your family. But what I want to know is why you are so quick to brush me off. I have apologized for participating in that rude wager. Have I otherwise offended you?"

"No."

"Am I repugnant to you?"

Corey looked away and shook her head. "Of course not."

"Then why?"

Corey wished she had a clear explanation for herself as well as for Matt. Everything in her head was all mixed up. Her need to provide for her parents. The resemblance of the Quorn Quartet's conduct to the disastrous deeds of her brother.

But above all, the thought of being an unloved wife.

A burden to him. A duty, as he had said last night. He would do his duty. That she could not endure.

Corey took a deep breath. "Marriage should not be forced on a couple, no matter what they have done."

"Corey, look at me. I have said, in the presence of witnesses, that I will marry you. Will you make a fraud of me?"

"I do not think we should suit, my lord. You would soon regret your offer."

"I am a better judge than you as to what my opinions would be."

Corey straightened her back and gritted her teeth. "Lord Matthew, if you have lost a wager because of my rebuff, I am truly sorry, though I will not try to compensate you for your losses."

His face reddened, whether from embarrassment or anger she did not know.

"Corey, I assure you there was no other wager."

"I think our conversation has come to its termination. If you will take the hamper in the rowboat with you, I will carry Henry's Zephyr back to the house. I am sure he will be distraught until he knows of its safety. I thank you very much for finding it."

She was surprised to see the look on his face. It appeared to be disappointment. Or perhaps he was simply thinking about rowing all the way back to the river.

He got to his feet, flinching a little as he stood. "I am not sure I agree we have had the last word on this subject, my dear. But I do agree you should take the sailboat back to Henry now. He deserves to know we found it."

"Then can I help you push the rowboat back in the water?"

"Not necessary. I will see you at the house later."

She watched him place the hamper on the floor-boards, shove the boat into the water, and hop in. The curious ducks paddled quickly out of the way as he took up the oars and pulled away from the bank.

Corey could not explain the tears in her eyes as she clasped the sailboat to her chest and headed away from the pond.

As she trudged toward the Hall, she could not throw off her unsettling thoughts about the future. As Matt had said, the dowager could spread scandalous stories about her character. She had dismissed the problem as ridiculous, but should she have been so quick to reject his concern?

She had been thinking of herself as a nobody on the London marriage mart. But ugly rumors could spoil her chance to find an employer who paid a reasonable wage. Or any employer at all.

She would fail in her attempt to settle her parents in Bath if no one would hire her. Thinking of her father watching another man in his pulpit made her want to sob out loud.

As bad as the prospect was, she would have to go to the dowager and beg her pardon, grovel to her. Even more to the point, perhaps help her gain Lord Matthew for Sophronia. Unless Sophy loved Alfred enough to defy her mother.

Matt tiptoed to the door of Elaine's boudoir and tapped lightly.

"Come."

He opened the door just a crack. "Lady Lodesham, it is Matthew. May I speak with you?"

"Of course. Come in, Matt. When did you return from the river? Have you seen Henry?"

"Not yet."

Elaine gazed up at him. "He is most anxious to thank you for finding his boat. I have never seen him so excited as when Corey came into the nursery with it. He had been inconsolable."

"I am glad he is happy."

"Please sit down. You look rather upset."

Matt pulled his chair close to her chaise. "I need to speak with you about Corey."

"Corey?"

"Yes. We have had a series of misunderstandings between us. She was understandably offended by the wager we made."

"Do you blame her, Matthew?"

"No. We men were entirely out of line. But I do not understand what she wants, what she is planning to do."

Elaine looked thoughtful. "I thought she was looking forward to going back to live with her parents. I know she writes to them twice a week and she often receives letters from her mother. But I am not sure. Of course, she has the makings of a good governess."

"A governess? What do you mean?"

"Never mind. I was just thinking that she has a talent with the children."

"Yes, Elaine, I agree. But why would she want to be a governess?"

"No, that is not what I meant. I was thinking, ah, I wish I had a governess who was as talented with children. I should not have said anything."

Matt did not believe her. "Lady Lodesham, are you hiding something? I suspect there is more to this."

Elaine's face clouded and she pressed her hands to her temples.

"Please, if there is any way I can help . . ." Matt let his voice fade.

"Oh, I should not tell you, but perhaps you can think of a solution." A tear spilled onto her cheek.

Matt handed her his handkerchief.

Elaine dabbed at her eyes. "It is a very complicated story. Corey wants to help her father and mother go to Bath for their retirement. They send every spare cent to her wastrel of a brother. She thinks if she finds a position as a lady's companion she will be able to pay for a house in Bath for them."

"But why would they let her do such a thing?

"She does not intend to tell them the whole story."

Matt could hardly believe his ears. "Sounds outlandish to me. Certainly her parents would not want to live on money earned by a daughter's labor."

Elaine sighed. "So I have told her. Not to mention that she would hardly make enough money for a place in Bath."

"That brother of hers, George Bransford, is a wastrel, all right. Accused of cheating at cards, if I remember correctly."

"Yes. He went to New York, then to Ontario, I believe."

Matt wished he could take a swing at the wretch. "He has been gone for several years and still cannot support himself? I have known men like George who believe that around the very next corner lies easy wealth. Some new scheme, some method of fleecing an honest tradesman. How could he be the brother of an upright and virtuous lady like Miss Bransford?"

"How could a mother like Lady Lodesham raise a wonderful and well balanced, good-humored man like Perry?" Elaine asked.

"There you have it. I suppose there are no sure things in this world, are there?"

"It makes me quake for my own darlings."

"If I may be so bold, Elaine, could you not have Miss Bransford stay here and continue to help you with the children? Perry might be able to assist her parents."

"Corey views such a plan as charity. She will not live off of pity, she says."

Matt could not picture Miss Bransford carrying the smelling salts for some elderly lady, acting like the dreaded Ingrey to keep tabs on every person in the household. It would ruin her spirit. Or she would give in to her tart tongue and be dismissed in nothing flat.

"I thank you, my dear, for telling me the whole story. I am still not quite sure I understand her view . . ."

"Nor do I."

Matt propped his leg up and lay back on the cushions of the barouche. His thinking was too fuzzy to comprehend and he hardly knew what to believe.

He had come here to Lodesham Hall to rediscover the carefree contests of his youth and to compete to win, regardless of his weak leg. But in a mere two weeks, his whole life had been turned upside down and inside out.

He did not care anymore about winning the contests, but he esteemed the companionship of his friends. For the first time, he had told another person about his hatred of war and in doing so, had clearly revealed his frailties, his limitations.

He developed a deep affection for a young lady, who apparently did not respect him as a man of integrity, though she was kind and compassionate when he spoke of the war.

He had offered her marriage, albeit under duress, and she had not only declined but apparently preferred to seek employment as a lady's companion to becoming his wife.

Up to now, marriage never appealed much to him, but the more time he spent with Corey, the more he thought it agreeable. He had spoken the other night out of gallantry and to defend Corey's honor. Now, he found he really did want to marry her. If he could convince her to have him, she would be an excellent wife and mother of their children. He would be more than happy to provide for her parents.

All in all, Matt viewed the world differently today than he had when he left London. What he thought he wanted to recover, the insouciance of youth, the carefree way they used to be—that would never happen. And he was not sorry.

He was different and happy in his new self.

Except for one thing: Corey's feelings for him. And those he was determined to change. Helping her mother and father was the key.

Corey and Sophronia were the only two up early on the morning of the ball, meeting over their morning chocolate in the breakfast room. Corey hoped to draw Sophy out and discover the nature of her affection for Alfred.

"Are you looking forward to returning to London, Lady Sophronia?"

"No. Not at all."

"But do you not enjoy the many entertainments, the balls, the theater?"

"Have you been to London for the Season, Miss Bransford?"

"Yes, I had one Season, the year that Perry and Elaine were betrothed. And please call me Corey."

"Thank you, Corey, and I am Sophy. I was only fifteen and not allowed to come to London. I remember the wedding, however. I thought it was very romantic. Elaine is so very beautiful."

"Yes. She was the toast of the Season. Perry was fortunate to win her hand."

Sophronia giggled. "I suppose that is true. My mother always talks of Elaine as the fortunate one. Were there many contenders for her hand?"

"Yes, but I do not believe she ever gave anyone a second look after Perry set his interest with her."

"Ah, yes, that is romantic."

Corey felt the time had come. "Perhaps you are in love right now?"

Sophy did not hesitate. "If you can keep my confidence, Corey, I think I am almost in love. I am growing fonder of Mr. Collingwood every day."

Corey took a deep breath. "I promise not to tell a soul, not even Elaine. Do you wish to marry him?"

Lady Sophronia gave a shy smile. "Mama would not approve, I fear. And I am not certain he loves me enough to brave her opposition." Sophy stared into the distance and sniffled. "Mama is impossible. I would almost marry Beelzebub himself to have my own establishment."

"She seems to have very strong opinions."

"Foolish ones. I've told Mama that I would do so

much better if she let me acquire some spectacles, but she says they would only make my eyes weaker. I do not believe it."

A wide smile suddenly brightened Sophy's face.

Corey turned to see Alfred take a chair at the table. She took a last sip of chocolate and made her excuses. They had eyes and ears only for each other. Corey thought how wonderful it would be to have someone you love look at you the way Alfred gazed at Sophy.

Corey had the answer to her question. She would have to gain the dreadful dowager's cooperation without helping her snag Lord Matthew for her daughter. And, somehow, she had to help Sophy and Alfred as well.

Corey's reflection in the cheval glass gave her a pang of nerves. Though Sawyer had adjusted the bodice of the silver-blue gown, Corey felt half-naked wearing it.

"Oh, miss," Fanny said with true admiration in her voice. "You look lovely."

"Is it not too low?"

"Not at all, miss. It is quite the fashion."

Corey tugged at the bodice but failed to bring it higher.

As Fanny finished her hair, weaving silver ribbons through the curls, Corey watched the light sparkling on the fabric that almost covered her breasts, which would draw even more attention to that part of her anatomy.

As soon as Fanny left, Corey reached into a drawer and found the four white silk roses she made from the silk she purchased in Dorchester. She pinned three in her hair and tucked the largest one into her bodice.

It did not cover as much of her bare skin as she hoped it would, but it nevertheless did fill the space between her breasts and might act as something of a deterrent to wandering eyes.

For several moments she stood and stared at her image in the looking glass. The person who stared back at her did not look like Cordelia Bransford at all.

When she came down the staircase, Cedric and Alfred waited at its base. Both of them almost jumped in surprise when they saw her. And both reached for her hand as she stepped off the last riser.

"Miss Bransford, you are l-looking stellar."

Cedric's gaze was fixed on her bodice. "Yes, I say, more than stellar."

Lord Matthew, nearby, turned and surprise showed on his face as well, but he was soon lost in the crush.

How silly men were, Corey thought, to be so bowled over by a little bare skin. From the second she stepped into the drawing room, she felt that every male eye in the room drilled into her chest. No one, not even Perry, met her gaze. All eyes focused below her chin and above the high waist of her gown.

She wanted to cross her arms over her chest and shout to all of them to look at Lady Sophronia, whose bosom was adorned with an elaborate display of jewels. Or at Elaine's ample décolletage. The face of the local squire grew so red she feared for his health. Though no remarks came to her ears, her imagination concocted enough randy comments to put her permanently to the blush. The evening seemed to stretch ahead forever. It could not conclude early enough, as far as she was concerned.

* * *

The ballroom glittered with hundreds of candles reflected in thousands of dangling crystals and a dozen gilded mirrors, reflected again in the jewels that glinted from ruby necklaces and sapphire bracelets, from diamond stickpins to Elaine's sparkling tiara.

Matt knew his face had revealed his surprise at Corey's gown. Though he noted her hair was done beautifully, his eye was drawn by the white rose in her bodice. He wanted to lean down and sniff it, though he knew it was silk and not real petals.

She wore her hair differently tonight, piled up on her head as if lifted off her shoulders, so that one's eyes were instantly drawn to the expanse of creamy skin, the swell of her breasts above the very low neckline of her gown. He could not take his eyes from the white rose between her breasts. He wished to bury his face in that rose, to feel her soft breasts, to smell her fragrance, as if that rose carried the scent of a real blossom. No, he mused, what he really wanted was to feel and experience the scent of her, to inhale her very essence.

He leaned back against the wall and let the truth sink into his brain. He had fallen deeply in love with Miss Cordelia Bransford. How lovely she was—soft, full lips that would feel velvety and smooth under his. Sparkling eyes, intense in their blueness. Cheeks of pale pink that would brighten when he whispered her name. And the rose nestled in her bosom. How could he live through the next few hours until he could be alone with her?

As the first sets formed, Matt watched Perry introduce Miss Bransford to a gentleman from the other side of Dorchester, whose name escaped him. Other than a satin waistcoat in too vivid a green, he looked perfectly acceptable for her partner, a fact which caused Matt a stab of irritation. Clearly Elaine had invited several eligibles to meet Miss Bransford, as well as several young ladies he, Alfred, and Cedric were supposed to entertain.

But Alfred was all wrapped up in dreams of Lady Sophronia. Cedric would gravitate, as always, to the prettiest girls.

Matt could not make his move until later in the evening when the dancing finished. In the meantime, he intended to keep Cordelia and her precious white rose in view at all times. He found the sight more intoxicating than the finest vintage.

Each dance set seemed doubly long, for he had to watch the others smile and laugh while he entertained a procession of young ladies on the sidelines. He told every one of them a different story about his bad leg. An accident while fencing at Angelo's. His horse falling on top of him. A misstep from a pier to a boat. It amused him to think up fresh atrocities while each miss sighed her condolences.

At last supper was announced and Matt neatly cut Miss Bransford from her partner and spirited her away down the corridor to a small salon.

"Where are you taking me?"

He rushed her away before anyone could stop them. "Just come along, if you please, Cordelia."

Matt led her to a small settee and sat down beside her. "I want you to marry me, Corey."

"What?"

"I am making you a formal proposal, Cordelia. Will you be my wife? I am prepared to go to Yorkshire immediately to speak to your father."

Instead of collapsing in his arms as he had expected,

she looked astonished. "I appreciate your kindness, Lord Matthew."

"Please, my dear, you must call me Matt."

"I cannot marry. I must try to help my parents. Their happiness means everything to me."

He leaned forward and took both her hands in his, preventing himself from kissing her only with the greatest of effort. "I can see that your parents have everything they need. I will find them a fine place in Bath and support them. I want to do that for you, Corey."

She shook her head slowly, and tears gleamed in her eyes. "Lord Matthew, I truly appreciate the assistance you suggest. But I cannot accept your offer." She stood, and without looking at his face, left the room.

Matt did not move for several minutes. His ears picked up the sound of the door closing. His heart still thumped in his chest. His leg still had that dull ache. His eyes took in his surroundings. His hand clenched and unclenched on his knee.

Still, his senses were entirely numb. He felt dead.

The possibility she would refuse him had never entered his mind. All day he had thought of himself as betrothed to Miss Cordelia Bransford. Even while prattling at those silly girls in the ballroom, in his mind he watched Corey at his estate, considered what renovations they might plan together, even envisioned the arrival of their children. He had taken on a whole new viewpoint; a new future had awaited.

Now the floor threatened to give way beneath him. The sky grew black with storms. He was entirely empty inside.

Thirteen

Matt's words were not what Corey wanted to hear. Pity was not a basis for a happy marriage. He had wealth; she had none. He felt sorry for her.

But it was a tempting thought. Married to Matt, she would have a home, probably children of her own. Her parents would be well provided for. She would have everything she needed. Except the love of a man to whom she had already lost her heart.

Could she survive a marriage in which the affection was entirely one-sided? Look at it from the other point of view, she told herself. If he adored me and I did not love him, would I marry him?

No. Never.

Corey started to her room, then thought better of the destination. If anyone came looking for her, it was certainly the first place they would try. She would not go to the rose garden, for surely other guests might stroll there for a breath of the beautifully scented air. She pulled Elly's soft, white cashmere shawl around her shoulders. Her little reticule and her fan bumped against her leg. It made her think of poor Lord Matthew, living with the constant pain of making his leg do its customary work without the support of the muscle that once had been able to carry his weight for all sorts of activities—fencing, boxing, astride a horse.

It had been kind of him to suggest marriage again. That very kindness made her love him more and thus heightened her reasoning that she could not marry him and live with him in a loveless situation. The more she loved him, the more impossible to think of being his neglected, unloved, miserable wife. She would always know he married her out of pity, sacrificing his own opportunity for love, the chance that someday he would meet a woman and fall truly in love. Though perhaps he would have grown fond of her in time, particularly if she bore him children.

She walked toward the kitchen garden but heard the whispers and laughter coming from behind its walls. Many of the servants who accompanied their families here were obviously making their own party near the service wing. She turned toward the stables, but again as she neared, she heard the voices of the grooms, apparently having a mug of ale and, from the sound of their cries, calling for the dice to be kind that evening.

A half-dozen carriages stood in the stable yard awaiting the homeward journey of their owners. Corey stopped and looked at them. If she climbed in one of them, she could sit in the dark, in perfect comfort, and have her little cry. But if, by chance, she fell asleep or failed to hear the approach of grooms preparing to harness the teams, how would she explain her presence in a stranger's equipage? But inside the carriage house, the Lodesham vehicles were empty and unused, sure to remain that way all night. No one would come near here at least until tomorrow.

She looked around—furtively, it would seem to anyone watching, she thought with a guilty pang. The stable door yielded to her tug and she stepped inside.

Faint smells of horses, of polished leather and axle grease, made her think of the livery stable at home where, when they needed a gig, she sometimes went with her father. Long ago, before George emigrated, they had given up their own stable of horses. Two hacks for riding and another pair to pull the small carriage in which her mother preferred to be driven. Since then, they had done without, hiring from time to time.

Corey let her eyes get used to the darkness, found a coach, and reached up on her tiptoes and opened the door. She clambered aboard, sinking into the comfortable cushions and curling up in the corner, cradling her cheek on her arm. How much money had it saved her family, having no horses? Papa had sold all four animals and the carriage to pay George's debts. She figured most of those debts came from gambling, that George's efforts at finding worthwhile employment were only stories he told to inspire the conveyance of more funds from her parents' meager savings. Sometimes she was sure her mother suspected. Other times, she thought her father must have put two and two together. But they never acknowledged George's deceits. They could not admit to themselves—nor especially to their daughter—that their only son was a useless failure.

Corey wished she could accept Lord Matthew's proposal so that her parents could be comfortable in their retirement. But she simply could not. A tear slipped down her cheek and she dug a handkerchief from her reticule to wipe it away.

If she had agreed to marry Lord Matthew, not only would her parents be provided for. She might also have a family, the children he desired. She would be the mother of her own darlings, little girls that might have his dark hair and piercing blue eyes. Little boys with whom he would sail boats in duck ponds and teach to fish and to row. For whom he would have Perry's men fashion a basket cart. For whom he would buy ponies.

For a moment she was mesmerized by the vision of these children, the boy older like Henry, the little girl all pink cheeks and messy curls like Gina. As their mama, Matt would give her tender looks of gratitude for his beloved children. But all that time, she would know that deep in his heart, he did not care for her in the way a man ought to desire a wife he adored. If she married him, she would never see the light of longing in his eyes the way Elaine saw passion burn in Perry's.

Strangely, now that she was alone in the velvety darkness, she did not feel like sobbing. She managed just that one little tear. Her need to sob out her disappointment, her regret, her grief, her sorrow, her anguish, her frustration, had faded to a dull ache in her midsection, a pressure in her chest, a heaviness in her heart.

If she confided these feelings to Elaine, her cousin would say she was a missish fool. Corey could hear Elaine's voice saying it. *You are a henwit if you do not marry Lord Matthew in a trice. Only a ninnyhammer of the first water would turn down an honest offer.*

Of course, Elaine could afford to be carefree and offhand about love. It was easy for her to discount its importance since for Elaine, there was no question that her husband adored her. Plus, nothing would please Elaine more than to see the dowager's schemes thwarted. How she would laugh!

Corey was so accustomed to the silence that she jumped when she heard a squeak. It sounded like someone was entering the carriage house. Her heart picked up an urgent beat. There was the unmistakable click of the latch closing. She heard footsteps and dared to peek out of the carriage. Whoever it was, he carried no lantern.

Her heart was literally in her throat when she made out his shape coming close and reaching for the handle of the brougham standing next to the very place she hid.

The words burst out of her involuntarily. "Lord Matthew!"

He whirled toward the sound. "Corey?"

"What are you doing here?" They spoke in unison.

He gave a little laugh, then opened the door of the carriage and peered inside. "May I join you?"

She pressed her hand on her heart to slow its pounding. Her voice was now barely a murmur. "Yes. I guess so. I am rather a trespasser here."

He stepped inside and she scooted over on the seat to make room for him. The light was so dim she could barely see him, but his presence filled the carriage and every nerve in her body seemed to tingle at his nearness.

He settled beside her, turned toward her, and seemed to smile. "No one else ever discovered my secret refuge, Corey."

"This is a secret refuge? I did not know it. I came here trying to find a place to be alone. Everywhere I went, there were guests and their servants."

"If you want me to leave you in solitude, I will do so."

"By no means. That is, ah, your company is welcome."

He gave a little laugh. "I wonder if the dowager will seek us out again. If so, my dear, I predict we will be in the soup for sure!"

"I have confidence she would never imagine us to be sitting in the carriage house. Why do you call it your refuge?"

Again, his little laugh came, but this time with a vinegary tone. "It was the only place I could find at home where I could get away from the constant supervision of my mother and my brother's wife. They thought I needed to be flat on my back in bed, eating only gruel, and suffering the leeches at least once a day. I had no strength after months of that regimen. When I finally managed to get away from them, Mama and the servants hunted me down like a pack of hounds. The empty carriages were my only sanctuary. So here at Lodesham Hall, I gravitated to the same refuge."

The melancholy in his voice stirred her deeply. Corey wished she could see more than the faint outlines of his face. She guessed he would have something of the same distant look in his eyes, the look she saw when he talked of Waterloo, a guarded look that had made her want to cradle him in her arms, press him to her breasts, and rock him like a baby. But instead of reaching for him, she twisted the strings of her reticule around her hands and folded them in her lap. "Your mother was trying to help, do you not agree?"

"Oh, yes, no doubt she was doing her best. And for the first month or two, rest was exactly what I needed. But the only thing that made me stronger was hard work. She saw my pain and wanted only to alleviate it. But leeches and laudanum were not the answer."

"But you still feel the pain."

"Yes. But eventually it will ease, and I am growing stronger every day."

"Will you return to the army?"

"No. I have neglected my estate ever since my father

made it over to me. The time has come for me to go there and put things in order. The hills of Somersetshire seem more and more to my liking. Once I thought it a rustic void, the back of beyond. Recently I have come to appreciate its appeal."

Corey looked down at her hands. "You are fortunate, Lord Matthew. You are loved by your family and you have a purpose to shape your future."

He reached for her fingers and untangled the strings from them, lifting her palm to his lips. "Corey, I want you to share that future with me."

Her heart tried to soar, but she willed it to slow its rapid beat. "Please do not begin that again, Matt. I have explained to you what I must do. Even if I fail, I will have done my utmost to take care of Father and Mother."

"I understand and honor your desire to help your parents. Nothing speaks better of your loyalty and devotion to them. As I told you, I am prepared to—"

"Stop! I cannot accept your charity, my lord. Remember how you felt when you arrived at Lodesham Hall. You told me you needed to win. To catch the most fish. To triumph over your friends. You needed to prove yourself to them. But even more, you were testing your inner self as well, were you not?"

"You are correct. But I have moved well beyond those foolish, childish aims. Not only were they aims I could never fulfill. They were empty goals, meaning nothing. I was wrong even to imagine it was important to defeat the others in competitions. What I know now is that the important thing is to enjoy my friends, accept their shortcomings, their imperfections, and their strengths, just as they accept me. This came not as a blinding flash of truth but gradually. I learned something about myself and about my closest friends."

"You are fortunate again, my lord, in your friends."

"Yes. What is important about the unwritten code of the true Corinthian is honor and loyalty, not victory at any price."

"My situation is entirely different."

"I disagree. The lesson should be the same for you as it is for me, Cordelia. It is the bond of love. When you love someone, you want to help that person . . ."

Corey felt a jolt like a lightning strike to her every nerve. *Love? He spoke of love?*

He went on speaking, his deep voice barely a whisper. ". . . to do whatever you can to alleviate one's burdens and one's worries."

Corey listened carefully for the mention of "love" again. "I do not wish to be the poor relation for whom everyone feels responsible. To accept charity from those who have resources when I am capable of doing for my own? I must try to work out my own problems."

He kissed her fingertips. "Corey, you made me a soothing ointment because you have a kind heart. You had no obligation. You chose to use your abilities with herbs. I have access to a house in Bath. Nothing would make me happier than to use my ability to set up your family and make them comfortable when your father leaves his church."

"How can you compare making a salve with taking on a financial obligation that could go on for years? The very idea is ludicrous."

He paid no regard to her objection. "Believe me, Corey, when I say it will give me great pleasure to do this for you. I do not see it as an obligation but as a kindness to the lady I love. I want to do this—"

Again, the word hit her like a crack of thunder in her ears. "What? What did you say?"

"It is not an obligation. It will give me the greatest satisfaction—"

"No! I mean about the lady you . . ." She could not repeat the very precious word she knew he had spoken. "About the lady you . . ."

He leaned close and lifted her chin with his forefinger. "The lady I adore?"

She let out her breath in a sigh of delight. "Ah, Matthew, please say that once more."

He put a hand behind her head and buried his fingers in her hair. "I love you."

Abruptly she felt a spate of tears fill her eyes and constrict her throat. Why was she crying now when he had spoken the words she longed to hear?

All she could do was murmur his name again and again. "Matthew. Matthew."

"Ah, my dearest, have you relented? Has my stubborn little darling finally seen the light?"

"How was I to know you cared for me as more than a poor chick who needed your benevolence?"

"Did not my very offer imply my love? Was Perry right all along? He once told me all females, even wives, require frequent declarations of love. I should have known I needed to say the words, Corey."

Corey spoke through her tears. "I thought you felt sorry for me. That was all you felt. To me, pity would not be a credible basis for marriage."

"I do not understand the rules of this matchmaking business, my darling. I have never before cared for anyone so deeply that I tried to propose marriage."

"Oh, Matt, I have been quite excessively thick-headed.

Do you see that I loved you too much to become your wife if you did not return my feelings?"

"I find your thoughts . . . confusing. Corey, if you love me, why would you refuse—"

"Shush, my lord. I would much rather hear your words again than try to explain my tortuous thinking."

She pressed against him and brought Matt's head to hers, opening her lips beneath his and tasting the passion she hoped to spend a lifetime exploring.

After the white rose had been crushed beyond redemption, Corey pulled her mouth from his. "Matt, can you grant me one more favor?"

"Anything, my darling."

"Will you help me convince the dowager to let Sophy marry Alfred?"

Matt squeezed her to him. "Of course, my sweet. I expect to spend a lifetime helping you do favors for others."

Her thanks were smothered by his kiss.

AUTHOR'S NOTE

Victoria Hinshaw is curently working on a Regency romance set in Suffolk, one of her favorite spots in England. She loves to hear from readers. Visit her at *www.victoriahinshaw.com* for articles on Regency topics, travel information and other material, and to e-mail Victoria. You may write to her c/o Zebra Books; please include a self-addressed stamped envelope if you wish a response.

More Regency Romance
From Zebra

Embrace the Romance of
Shannon Drake

BOOK YOUR PLACE ON OUR WEBSITE AND MAKE THE READING CONNECTION!

We've created a customized website just for our very special readers, where you can get the inside scoop on everything that's going on with Zebra, Pinnacle and Kensington books.

When you come online, you'll have the exciting opportunity to:

- View covers of upcoming books

- Read sample chapters

- Learn about our future publishing schedule (listed by publication month *and author*)

- Find out when your favorite authors will be visiting a city near you

- Search for and order backlist books from our online catalog

- Check out author bios and background information

- Send e-mail to your favorite authors

- Meet the Kensington staff online

- Join us in weekly chats with authors, readers and other guests

- Get writing guidelines

- AND MUCH MORE!

**Visit our website at
http://www.kensingtonbooks.com**